YOUR

A Novel By

Adrienne Thompson

Pink Cashmere Publishing

Cover Design by Adrienne Thompson

Cover Art from dreamstime.com

All rights reserved.

This book or any portion thereof may not be reproduced or used in any manner whatsoever without the express written permission of the publisher except for the use of brief quotations in a book review.

This is a work of fiction. Names, characters, businesses, places, events and incidents are either the products of the author's imagination or used in a fictitious manner. Any resemblance to actual persons, living or dead, or actual events is purely coincidental.

Printed in the United States of America

First Printing 2013

Copyright © 2013 Adrienne Thompson

ISBN: 0988871343

ISBN-13: 978-0-9888713-4-2

Also by Adrienne Thompson

The *Bluesday* Series:
Bluesday
Lovely Blues
Blues In The Key Of B

The *Been So Long* Series:
Rapture
Been So Long
Little Sister
Been So Long 2 (Body and Soul)

When You've Been Blessed (Feels Like Heaven)
See Me
Just Between Us (Inspiring Stories by Women) *– as a contributor*

This is book number ten!! All I can say is PRAISE GOD!! I am so grateful for the blessings He's showered upon me! God, You are so good to me and for that I humbly say, THANK YOU!

A special thank you to Author Teresa D. Patterson, Author Cathy Jo G, Author Janice Ross, Author TM Brown, Author Julia Press Simmons, Author Tamika Christy, Author Tremayne Moore, Author Selena Haskins, Author Sandra Hall, Author Barbara Joe Williams, Author Karen E. Quinones Miller, Author Deidra DS Green, Author Nicole Dunlap, Author Stacy Campbell, Author Kim Beverly, Author Phoenix Brown, Author Nakia Laushaul, and Author Kimberly Matthews for your support and for sharing your unique talents with me and the rest of the world.

A special shout out to the following readers:

Debi Gonsalves, Sophie Sealy, Mia Danielle, Dale Fields-Glivings, Leslie Hudson, Saundra Harden, Peace Still, Jamie Young, Standifur-Curry Cynthia, Sharon Evans, Lareeta Robinson, Monica Meadors, Alicia Smith-Perdue, Tracy Bell, Nikkie Frazier Johnson, Delice Currie, La'ChaCha Crawford,

Marsha Brown, Las Gray, Michelle Burns, Stephanie Shelton, Channon Cook-Horne, Tonja Tate, Toshona Carter, Yola Yen, Juanesia Walker, E Bidd, LaSonya Artis Woodom, Lady K, Singlefabulous Andlovingit, Karen McCollum Rodgers, Book Referees, Orsayor Simmons, the Sistahs of Color Reading Group, and the In the Company of My Sisters Book Club. I KNOW I've forgotten someone. Please, *please* charge it to my head and not my heart for I thank God for each and every one of you!

There are three things that amaze me— no, four things that I don't understand:

how an eagle glides through the sky,

how a snake slithers on a rock,

how a ship navigates the ocean,

how a man loves a woman.

Proverbs 30:18-19 NLT

SOUNDTRACK PROVIDED BY SADE:

"YOU'RE NOT THE MAN"

"BE THAT EASY"

"FEAR"

"GIVE IT UP"

"IMMIGRANT"

"DIAMOND LIFE"

"SMOOTH OPERATOR"

"FLOW"

"SKIN"

"I NEVER THOUGHT I'D SEE THE DAY"

"EVERY WORD"

"KISS OF LIFE"

"LOVERS ROCK"

"THE SWEETEST TABOO"

"NO ORDINARY LOVE"

SOUNDTRACK CONTINUED:

"NOTHING CAN COME BETWEEN US"

"BY YOUR SIDE"

"IS IT A CRIME?"

"IT'S ONLY LOVE THAT GETS YOU THROUGH"

"THE MOON AND THE SKY"

"HANG ON TO YOUR LOVE"

"TURN MY BACK ON YOU"

"IN ANOTHER TIME"

"SOMEBODY ALREADY BROKE MY HEART"

"SOLDIER OF LOVE"

"PARADISE"

ONE

"YOU'RE NOT THE MAN"

I rolled over in the bed after a short nap, opened my eyes, and nearly jumped out of my skin. For a brief moment, I'd forgotten that Darius was lying next to me. The sight of him lying there asleep with his mouth wide open startled me.

I eyed him with disgust as I tried to ease out of bed undetected. I slid and slid until my feet finally reached the floor, then I tiptoed through the cluttered efficiency apartment into the bathroom. I peered into the smudged mirror and wondered to myself, *What are you doing, Marli Meadows? Why are you here with him?* I shook my head as if the mere action could erase my relationship with Darius Cotton right out of my life.

I squatted over the toilet and relieved myself, afraid to sit on the seat. Knowing Darius, there was no telling how many other butts had been on that seat. I turned the water in the faucet on to a slow trickle, still not wanting to awaken Darius, and washed my hands. I dried them with some toilet paper and then quickly pulled my underwear and work uniform back on and slowly opened the creaky bathroom door.

I exited the bathroom and found Darius sitting on the side of the bed, lighting up a blunt. *Dang!* I thought, *if I don't get out of here quick, I'll be smelling just like that stuff and probably get a contact high. It'd be my luck for them to pop up with a random drug test at work and that crap'll show up.*

"You leaving, baby?" he grunted between drags. He rubbed his hand across his bare chest and stretched. I eyed his nakedness as I walked back into the room.

"Yeah, it's already eleven. I gotta go home and get some rest for work tonight," I answered as I gathered up my purse and slipped on my shoes.

With a lopsided grin on his face, he revealed two rows of shiny gold teeth and said, "Yeah, cause you know if you stay here you gon' have to put in some more work, huh?"

Ugh, I thought. "Yeah, well, I'll talk to you later, Darius."

"A'ight, come give me a kiss, boo."

I swallowed hard. I know this sounds strange considering the fact that I'd just had sex with him, but the thought of kissing him really didn't appeal to me. It took all I had in me to walk over to him, bend over, and plant a kiss on his dark lips.

He swatted my butt. "A'ight girl, I'll holla at you later. Don't work too hard tonight."

I nodded. "I won't. Bye, Darius."

"Bye, Mar-lay."

I shook my head as I closed the door behind me. We'd been "seeing" each other for nearly two years, and he still mispronounced my name. Well, it was either that or he was just so country that it *sounded* like he was mispronouncing it. Whichever was the case, it was irritating.

I walked down the steep stairs from Darius's apartment out onto the parking lot. I unlocked and then climbed into my Toyota Camry which was parked right next to Darius's souped-up Chevy Caprice. I rolled my eyes at the repeated Louis Vuitton logos covering his car. I backed out of my space and glanced at his license plate which read, SMOKONE. I sighed as I pulled off the lot.

One might wonder what a thirty-three-year-old registered nurse was doing with a twenty-seven-year-old drug dealer, and the only answer I can provide is, *I don't know.* Okay, well, that's a lie. I actually *do* know. See, the thing is, Darius was basically a sex machine. He was actually probably the best I'd ever had up to that point, and believe me, after my divorce, I had plenty of guys.

Too many to name.

The biggest problem with Darius was that he shared his talents with most of the plus-sized female population of our little city, though he claimed I was his only girl. Well, that and that little fact about him smoking and selling dope.

I pulled into the driveway of my modest home, stumbled through the front door, and collapsed onto the couch without bathing or changing my clothes. I'd worked twelve hours at the hospital on the previous night and had another twelve hours of work ahead of me. So I decided to get a little shut-eye before my 18-year-old daughter, Tiffany, made it home from school.

I glanced at the clock on the wall and squeezed my eyes shut. After about ten minutes, I finally drifted off to sleep, only to be awakened by the ringing of my cell phone.

Dang it! I peered at the screen through one open eye and let it roll to voice mail. It was my best friend, Carla. *I'll call her back later.*

I sniffed at the collar of my scrub top and inhaled a scent that was a combination of Darius's cheap cologne *and* his cheap marijuana. I shut my eyes and drifted back off to sleep.

~*~

I sat across from Gail, the nurse I was relieving, and listened as she gave me report on the six patients I'd be caring for over the next twelve hours. I nodded and smiled and jotted down notes, but honestly, I was still tired from the previous night and really wished I didn't have to work. When report was finally over, I grabbed my stethoscope and headed down the hall to check on my patients.

Finding everyone breathing and in no distress, I returned to the nurses' station and checked for any new doctor's orders before I began to write my assessments.

Every night it was the same routine, and although I enjoyed caring for the patients, it was all becoming really mundane. I'd been a nurse for six years, and it was time for a break or a change or something. I just needed *something* new in my life. For me it was work, work, sleep, sleep, and occasionally church. I had no real social life because I was simply too tired. I did try my best to make Tiffany's school events, but working twelve hours three to four nights every week usually prohibited my attendance.

The night was pretty uneventful, and somehow I managed to stay alert and awake. Well, that might've had something to do with me calling Carla whenever I felt a little sleepy. She worked at the same hospital and on the same shift as me, but as a respiratory therapist. We talked off and on for most of the night about everything and nothing in particular, and when the end of my shift finally arrived, I was more than relieved and ready to leave.

I was so exhausted; I nearly had to drag myself out of the hospital and onto the parking deck. Once inside my car, I uttered a quick prayer for a safe drive home. I couldn't wait to climb into my bed.

I shook my head as I thought about the fact that this cycle would start all over again in twelve hours—another grueling shift and another exhausted ride home. I would've given anything to break up the monotony of my life.

Anything.

TWO

"BE THAT EASY"

"I missed you," Darius said through a puff of smoke.

I turned over in the bed and faced him. Darius was an oddly handsome man. His black-brown eyes were huge and round, his nose was wide, and his lips were ridiculously full. Something about those oversized features appealed to me. He was medium brown-skinned and he wore his coarse hair in neat cornrows. He was about 5'6" tall with a stocky build.

"You just saw me a coupla days ago," I replied.

"Yeah, but I really be missing you when you ain't here. I like having you around."

I was a little puzzled because in the two years Darius and I had been in this "relationship," we'd never done much talking, and here he was, actually expressing his feelings. "Well, I enjoy our time together, too," I said.

He took another drag and sucked in a breath. "Yeah, I mean, sometimes I think about you being a nurse and everything and I wonder why you with me. You know? I mean, I know I ain't educated like you, but I like what we got together," he grunted as he exhaled a cloud of marijuana smoke.

"Yeah, it's a good arrangement," I agreed, trying to hold my breath.

"Uh, Marlay, you think maybe we could like take things to the next level?"

Dang, we're having sex on the regular. How much farther could we go? "What do you mean?" I asked, trying not to sound annoyed. But all of this talking was beginning to get on my nerves.

He sat up in the bed and set his joint in an astray on the cluttered nightstand. "Well, you know. Maybe we could move in together. I could pay most of the bills. Business is pretty good right now. Or I could get a real job and go legit if you want."

"Um, Darius, that's not even my house. It's my family's, and they'd go through the roof if you moved in. Plus, you know I have a daughter. I can't be shacking up over her."

"Ain't that girl 'bout to graduate? Hell, she grown. And we can get another place together."

"Are you serious? You ready to hang your player hat up for me?" I asked skeptically. That would be hard to believe.

"Look, baby… I been thinking a lot lately. I'm ready to settle down, maybe even get a real job, like I said. Maybe it's time for me to get my life straight. You the only one I can do that with. You the smartest woman I know and you got a lot going for you."

Translation: I have the best job of the women you've been sleeping with. "I see. Well, I just don't know, Darius. I'll have to think about it."

"A'ight, I got you. But I'm being for real, Marlay. I'm ready for us to really be together."

I nodded.

I lay there for a few moments and then reached over and rubbed his bare chest. He smiled, and before long, we were on our third round. A couple of hours later, I left his place, satisfied but confused. His words had made me see him in a different light—that is, if he really meant what he was saying. I was surprised by his offer, and although I'd only ever thought of him as a booty call and I wasn't in love with him or anything, I was actually considering it. I guess I was looking for most anything to shake up my world. Living with Darius would be nothing if not interesting.

~*~

On Saturday, a little over a week before Tiffany's graduation, my dad invited us to his house for dinner. He lived in a huge house a few miles outside of town with his wife and daughter, and I was pretty sure he had a gift for Tiffany. I looked out the window of Tiffany's yellow VW Bug and sighed as she drove down the rural road. I was definitely not looking forward to this visit.

Sensing my tension, Tiffany glanced at me with almond-shaped eyes that were duplicates of mine and asked, "You all right, Mama?"

I looked over at her and smiled. "I'm okay, just not too excited about this little trip."

"Mama, you've gotta stop letting gramps get to you. I mean, just ignore him or tell him off, but stop stressing. You're gonna make yourself sick."

She was right but I really didn't want to discuss it. I shook my head. "It's not that simple, Tiff. You wouldn't understand."

"I understand that you're a grown woman, and you don't have to answer to anyone. You can't let your parents control you forever."

I looked over at her and frowned. "They don't control me, Tiffany. Anyway, watch what you say to me. I *am* still your mother."

"I'm sorry. I just hate to see you like this. You look like you're about to have a panic attack over seeing your own father. It shouldn't be like that."

I dropped my eyes and nodded. "Yeah, you're right. It shouldn't."

The rest of the ride was spent listening to the radio. When Tiffany finally pulled into my father's driveway, I closed my eyes and took a deep breath. *Here we go.*

We walked up to the front door and as Tiffany rang the doorbell, she offered me an encouraging smile. I returned hers with a weak smile of my own and then pasted on a fake one for my stepmother, Carmen, as she opened the front door.

"Hello, girls," she said in her usual, haughty tone.

Clad in an expensive-looking, black, wrap-style dress and killer gold heels, the statuesque Carmen led us through the house and into the dark den, her expensive perfume leaving a trail behind her.

"Sugar, your girls are here," she announced in an exaggerated "Southern belle" accent that she reserved for my father.

My father stood up and, with a smile on his face, pulled Tiffany into a hug so tight, I was afraid he would crush her thin frame. Then he turned to me and hugged me, too. Things always began like this with us—nice and cordial. But before the visit was over, things always, *always* went south.

"Hey, Dad," I said softly.

"Marli," he said, acknowledging my greeting. He turned his attention to Tiffany. "Tiff-Tiff! How's grandpa's girl?"

Tiffany flashed him her best smile. "I'm well, how are you?"

He laughed heartily. "That's my girl! Manners of a queen. I'm good, baby. Real good. Come, let me show you what I'm looking at here."

With that, they spent the bulk of the visit discussing some legal website. At sixty years old, my father was still the head of his own law firm, and it thrilled his soul that Tiffany would be following in his footsteps. My dad, Marlon White, Esq., was one of the most successful lawyers in the state and had served on several prestigious boards and committees. He had been grooming Tiffany for a career in law for as long as I could remember, and he was willing to do anything to make sure his wish came to fruition, including paying for her education.

It was my father who'd insisted that she attend a private school, and it was him who'd paid for it. Now he'd chosen for her to attend Spelman and had already paid her first year's tuition. She was to move the week after graduation to begin summer school. My father adored her above anyone else.

I sat quietly on the leather sofa and watched the interaction between my father and my daughter and felt a pang of jealousy. I'd often wished that my dad and I had a closer relationship, but I knew the choices I'd made in life had prevented it. I'd embarrassed him, and that was something he did not easily forgive.

I was so deep in thought that I didn't realize Carmen was talking to me. Actually, I think I'd blocked out the fact that she was still in the room.

"Marli?" she repeated.

"Oh, yes, did you say something?"

"Well, I was asking how your work was going. Are you still at the hospital?"

I nodded. "Oh, yeah, I am. It's going okay. Nursing is always hard work, though."

My father shook his head. "There's no reason for you to be doing that work. You're smart enough to be the CEO of that place. You just made the wrong choices in life," he said without turning away from the computer. Only in my family would being an RN be considered an underachievement.

"Well, I did the best I knew how," I rebutted.

"If that was your best, I'd hate to see your worst."

Tiffany jumped into the conversation. "Grandpa, did I tell you I got another scholarship?"

Well, that took the spotlight off of me, thank goodness. I spent the rest of the time before dinner in silence, but things only got worse once we were all seated around the dinner table. There we were joined by my half-sister, Justine, who was my father and Carmen's only child together. She was three years younger than Tiffany.

After my father said grace, we all began eating a meal of grilled salmon, wild rice, and mixed vegetables. Halfway through the meal, my father started in on me again.

"Marli, are you enjoying the salmon?" he asked.

I knew that was a trick question, but I answered it anyway. "Yes, sir. It's really good."

"Well, I wanted to have barbeque, but with your weight and all, I decided salmon would be better," he replied.

I nearly choked, but then again, I don't know why I was surprised. My father had always been fixated with my weight—even when I weighed far less than the 260 pounds I weighed at that moment. I'd never been skinny. I'd never *be* skinny. I'd accepted that. He wouldn't.

"I hate salmon," Justine said matter-of-factly.

"Well, Justine, we have to consider your sister's health," my father said.

"Whatever," was Justine's reply as she rolled her eyes.

My father turned his and everyone else's attention back to me. "Well, Marli, Tiffany'll be moving in a couple of weeks. What are you going to do with yourself?"

I shrugged. "I really don't know. It'll be weird being alone in that house."

"Are you dating anyone?" Carmen asked.

I nodded. "Well, yeah, I've been seeing someone."

My father snapped his head in my direction. "Well, you better not be thinking about shacking up with someone in that house. Tiffany will still be coming home for breaks, and you know that any man you're with will only try to get to her."

"What?!" I shrieked, my eyes bugged.

"You heard me. No man will just want to be with you. They'll use you to get to your daughter. The only man that needs to be in that house is her father."

"Daddy, Tim and I are divorced and have been for years now! And you don't even *like* him."

"I don't like him, but he's Tiffany's father, and I know he'd never harm her. I can't say that for whatever thug you're hanging around with."

"Why do I have to be with a thug?" I asked. Yeah, Darius was a thug, but he didn't know that for sure.

"Because who else would want you? Look at you," he said with a straight face.

After a moment of uncomfortable silence, I said, "Wow, okay. Um, thanks for dinner. I think I'll be leaving now." I turned to Tiffany who looked absolutely livid. "Tiff, you can get your gift or whatever. I'll be waiting in the car."

I excused myself from the table and headed out to the car that had been a sweet sixteen gift to Tiffany from my father. I slid into the passenger's seat and as hard as I fought, lost the battle with my tears. After a few minutes, Tiffany and her gift—a huge check—arrived, and we headed back home. All the while, I wished I could just run away.

THREE

"FEAR"

Sunday morning, I decided to go to church with Tiffany. While she rarely missed a Sunday, it was sometimes difficult for me to attend due to my work schedule. So when I happened to be off, I tried to take advantage of the opportunity. I woke up early, fixed us a light breakfast, and poured my body into a pair of black slacks and a white blouse. I picked out my short afro and pulled on a pair of black flats which, along with a pair of silver hoop earrings, completed the outfit. I felt good as we headed out to church.

We pulled onto the lot and a smile spread across my face. There was nothing like seeing everyone stepping out in their Sunday best. The women in their dress-suits and flamboyant matching hats, the men in their nice suits, complete with tie and freshly shined shoes, and the little girls in ruffles and bows, signaled that it was definitely Sunday and it was definitely time for church. I'd been attending Bayou Chapel Missionary Baptist Church since I was a little girl, and it was home to me. Honestly, I couldn't see myself anywhere else.

I parked my car in my usual spot, on the right side of the church, and walked into the sanctuary. I took a seat on my regular pew, the next-to-the-last one to the right of the pulpit. From that seat, I had a full view of both the pastor and the choir. And no one would want to miss the choir. They always *threw down*!

I took a deep breath and released it as I settled into my seat and looked over the bulletin. I was glad to be at church, but I knew I'd need to say a special prayer. There was a lot going through my mind—more than I cared to admit—and I needed to think and mull it all over.

It wasn't long before the music began, signaling the start of worship service. I stood to my feet, clapped my hands, and swayed to the music. The opening song was one of my favorites, "If I Be Lifted Up." I smiled and sang along with the choir, although I couldn't carry a tune even if my life depended on it.

Worship service lasted the usual two hours, following the strict schedule of praise and worship, devotion, announcements, more music, offering, sermon, and invitation to discipleship. All in all, it was a good service, and I left there feeling very refreshed.

Afterward, Tiffany and I headed to my mom's house. She and her second husband attended Bayou Baptist, too, but hadn't made it to church on this particular Sunday. We were to have dinner with them as we did most Sundays after church.

On the way there, Tiffany decided to bring up our disastrous dinner with my father.

"Mom, are you okay? I mean, after yesterday?" she asked. I glanced at her and could see the concern written all over her face.

"I'm fine. I'm used to it," I answered with a shrug.

"I know, but I hate it when he talks to you like that. I don't know how you can take it. It burns me up!"

"Yeah… well, that's the nature of our relationship. I've disappointed him in a lot of ways, and he's not ever gonna to let me forget it. I just try to make my interactions with him few and far between."

"Yeah, and now, with me graduating, you're having to see him more often. I'm sorry."

I looked over at her and shook my head. "It's not your fault. I think you're the one thing he believes I got right. Anyway, let's just try to enjoy dinner with Mama. Don't worry about it."

Tiffany nodded in response, and a few minutes later, we arrived at my mother's house. My mother lived in a home a little larger than mine on the opposite side of town. It was the second home that she and my father purchased together during their marriage. The one I lived in was their starter home.

I knocked and waited until my mother finally opened the door. She was wearing a flowing, red-print caftan which almost disguised the extra weight she was carrying. On her head, she wore a matching scarf. In her hand was her usual dinnertime glass of wine. Edna, or

Professor Edna Gray, as she preferred to be called, hugged us and then led us into her overly decorated living room. My mother was a collector of many things, including all types of décor.

Fred, her husband, smiled and greeted me and Tiffany with a boisterous, "There they are! How y'all doing?"

Tiffany and I responded with a chorus of, "Hey, Mr. Freddie."

We sat and talked with Fred, who was always good for a friendly conversation, until Mama announced that dinner was ready. Now, don't get it twisted, my mother does *not* cook. Never has. I actually grew up on hamburgers and fried chicken—a fact that would explain my weight issues. So dinner was catered by Bill's Fried Chicken, a local favorite.

Bill's was true to the words of its slogan: "So Good, You'll Think Grandma Made It." Sunday's dinner with Mama was much more relaxed than Saturday's dinner with my dad, but true to form, Mama eventually let the liquor take over her inhibitions and her true feelings about me began to surface.

"So, Marlena Marie," she slurred. "Whatcha been up to? Got a new man?"

I wasn't sure how to answer that question. Mama knew about Darius and had even met him once. She didn't approve of him, of course, but in her mind, any man was better than no man at all.

"Um, no," I answered.

Her mouth spread into a knowing smirk. "Mm-hmm. Still with that little thug boy, huh?"

I sighed. "I'm still seeing Darius, if that's who you're referring to."

She shook her head. "Well, I guess if you can't do any better. I've never had that problem, *as you know*. Always had good, hard-working men in my life." She reached over and patted Fred on the arm. "You've gotta lose that weight, baby girl. Your choices are just so limited by your size. When I was your age, I was a perfect ten," she said and then took a bite out of a chicken leg.

Now, that was a lie. I'd seen pictures of my mother taken when she was my age. She might not have been as heavy as I was, but she was no ten. I knew if I tried to argue the fact with her, she'd say I was disrespecting her. So I held my tongue.

"Now, Edna, leave her alone," Fred said.

She held a hand up at him. "Hush, Fred." She turned to me and continued. "It's the truth. Look at Tiffany. She's beautiful and she'll have no trouble finding a good husband. You shoulda just stayed with Tim. At least he had a good job."

I dropped my head and stared at my plate for a moment. I guess it had slipped her mind that Tim actually left *me*, not the other way around. I drew in a breath and exhaled. "Mama, I respect your opinion, but I'm fine, really. I'm not worried about having a man."

"Mm-hmm. That's what everyone who doesn't have a man says. But I'm here to tell you. *You* need a man."

That was all I could take, because I knew things were only going downhill from there. I knew my mother too well. She was *always* right in her own mind, and she *always* got the last word.

I placed my napkin on the table. "Well, I guess this is just the weekend for me to leave the table early. I think I'll excuse myself now."

I stood to leave, but as I made my way toward the dining room entrance, she spoke again. "And by the way, if you're ever gonna get married again, you're gonna have to raise your standards. That thug just will not do. I mean, he's okay for a good time, but he won't be eating at *my* table."

I sighed. "Mama, who said anything about marrying him? Who said I *ever* want to get married again?" I shook my head and tried to leave the room before she could answer. I wasn't fast enough.

"Well, I guess he's better than nothing. At least with Tiff off at college you don't have to worry about him molesting her," Mama said.

Tiffany gasped.

I stopped in my tracks and turned to look at my mother. "What are you talking about? I've never been worried about that. He's never even been alone with her."

Mama smirked. "Well, you *should've* been worried. Now, I'm the one who didn't have to worry about anything like that when I was dating after *my* divorce. After all, you *never* looked like Tiff. Who was going to molest a fat girl?"

I stood frozen for a moment. Had she really just basically said I was too unattractive to be molested? What did that even mean? Was that a good thing or a bad thing?

At a total and complete loss for words, I turned and walked out of the house. Once inside my car, I cranked the engine and blasted the music on my radio to drown out the echo of my mother's words in my head. There were times when I came as close as one could get to despising my parents. This was one of those times.

As the music began to calm me, I sat and waited for Tiffany. She knew the drill. We'd been through this several times. She'd say her goodbyes and then join me in the car where she knew I'd be waiting for her.

I closed my eyes, tapped my fingers on the steering wheel, and nodded my head to an old En Vogue song and pretty soon, she did just as I expected, but this time, Fred was right behind her. As Tiffany climbed into the passenger's seat, Fred leaned over and tapped on my window.

I rolled the window down and looked up at him. "Yes, sir?"

"Hey, Marli. Now you know your Mama didn't mean all that stuff she said. That was just the liquor talking," he said in his usual calm, gentle voice.

I shook my head. "It's okay. I'm used to it. You don't have to try to make me feel better. I know exactly how both of my parents feel about me. I always have. I just wish they wouldn't say that stuff in front of my child."

He reached inside the car and patted my hand. "Now, don't you get down on yourself. You're a good person, an angel. Tiffany knows that. Don't let anyone tell you any different, not even your mama and daddy. And remember, God loves you. To Him, you are absolutely perfect."

I offered him a weak smile and a nod. "Okay, thanks. I really needed to hear that."

He smiled and backed away from the car, allowing me to leave the driveway. I rode in silence, contemplating the events of the weekend and wishing there was something I could do to change things. But I just couldn't see how things could, or would, ever change for me.

~*~

Monday night was an especially grueling one at the hospital. As the only RN on the unit that night, I was assigned as charge nurse by default, making me responsible for the care of all twenty-four patients on the floor, six of whom I cared for directly with the other eighteen split amongst three LPNs. It took me forever to complete and then chart assessments on all of the patients and after that, I had to pass meds and take care of any wound care that was ordered. By midnight, I was already exhausted—a fact that I shared with Carla. But that didn't keep her from visiting my unit on her break.

"Shouldn't you be in your area?" I asked as she took a seat next to me at the nurses' station.

Carla gave me an exaggerated roll of her eyes. "Girl, *please*. That's why they gave me this tracking device." She held up her locator badge. "Anyway, I'm entitled to two breaks and a lunch per shift. This is break number two."

I nodded. "I hear you. This is break number one for me. I think they're trying to kill me."

"Well, that's why I came down here. I wanted to talk to you about something."

I sighed and braced myself for whatever she was about to say. Carla was very good at giving people her unsolicited, no-holds-barred take on their lives—mine included. But right at that moment, I was not in the mood for it. "What's up, Carla?"

She smiled. "Now, don't be like that, Marlena Marie. It's a business proposition. I think you'll like it."

I raised my eyebrows. "Like what?"

"Well, you remember Dana Cobb, right?"

"Dana from high school? Yeah, I remember her. She was always pretty smart."

Carla nodded. "Yeah, she was. Well, she's running a medical staffing agency now. I ran into her the other day, and she says she's trying to staff a hospital in St. Louis."

"Okay?"

"Evidently, there's a strike or something going on, and they're willing to pay top dollar."

"For respiratory therapists?"

"*And* nurses. We're talking thousands of dollars per week. It's a three-month assignment."

"Well, are you going?" I asked.

She smiled brightly. "Yep, and I want you to come with me."

I shook my head. "You know I can't leave here, Carla."

She cocked her head to the side and put her hands on her hips. "Why? Give me one valid reason."

"Tiff—"

"Tiff is leaving for Atlanta in a week."

"Well, you know I can't fly. They'll try to make my big tail buy two tickets." I was only half-joking.

"We can drive, Marli. It's only six hours away. They'll give us a living allowance and set us up in an apartment. Everything is pretty much laid out for us. Plus, with the money you'll earn, you'll be well on your way to buying your own house. I know you're tired of being in your parents' place. You say so all the time."

"Yeah, but I just don't know. Carla, you know me. I'm not big on changes like this."

Carla leaned forward and looked me straight in the eye. "Marli, you're thirty-three years old, and you've been unhappy for most of your life. Don't you think it's time for a change?"

I looked down at the gray nurses' station desk. "I... I just don't know if I can do it. Move away to some strange place, away from everything I've ever known?"

She leaned back. "Well, I'm leaving in three weeks. Just think on it for a while. If you decide to go, let me know in a week or so."

I nodded. "Okay."

FOUR

"GIVE IT UP"

It was Friday night. Graduation night—a night I had both anticipated and dreaded for a long time. I was thrilled that my only child was graduating from high school and at the top of her class, no less. But the thought of an evening in the presence of both of my parents *and* my ex-husband was not something I looked forward to. It was the last thing I needed, but it was something I knew I had to do.

I sat in the Pine Bluff Convention Center arena next to Carla and wondered where my mom and dad and Tim, along with their respective spouses, were sitting. That was one of the good things about any local high school graduation—it was always packed, and unless people arrived as a group, there was no guarantee of them sitting together. Thank goodness for that.

After a twenty-minute wait, which Carla filled with chatter about her upcoming trip to St. Louis, the graduates began to file into the arena, prompted by the opening strains of "Pomp and Circumstance." I, along with everyone else in the room, stood to my feet as the burgundy-robed teenagers slowly marched in, all wearing bright smiles. They exuded hope for the future. I smiled as I spotted Tiffany leading the line. I nudged Carla and pointed Tiffany out to her. Carla, always the vocal one, yelled Tiffany's name and waved at her. Tiffany looked up, spotted us, and waved back.

After the procession, everyone took their seats. I settled into my seat and eyed the entrance that was nearest me. Although he wasn't around Tiffany much, Darius had promised to be at her graduation. I'd texted the section I was sitting in to him but had received no reply. *Maybe he hasn't checked his phone*, I thought.

As I sat through the various elements of the ceremony, I thought about Darius's proposition. I'd actually almost decided to let him move in. No, I didn't love him and sometimes he really irritated me, but I didn't relish the thought of living alone once Tiffany left for Atlanta. I guess that really wasn't a good enough reason to move in with someone, but I'd never been a great decision-maker, and Lord knows I didn't have a history of basing my decisions on the right things.

When it was finally time for Tiffany to recite her valedictory speech, I thought I'd burst with pride. After all I'd been through—having her at fifteen, marrying at seventeen, divorcing at twenty-five, and then raising her on my own—she'd turned out pretty good. No, she'd turned out rather excellent, despite the dysfunction that surrounded her. I knew I had God to thank for that. He'd always watched over us, even when I didn't realize or deserve it.

My eyes were glued to her as she spoke, and when she was

finished, Carla and I gave her a standing ovation.

Tiffany's name was the first one called during the awarding of the diplomas, and I thought I'd scream myself hoarse. I stood, applauded, and smiled as the other names were announced, all 300 of them, one by one. Once everyone had their diplomas in hand, and after the ritualistic rotating of the tassels, the class was presented and the audience converged on the arena floor, each person searching for his or her graduate.

Carla hugged me, handed me an envelope for Tiffany, and then left. I made my way to the floor, weaving through the maze of well-wishers until I finally reached Tiffany, who was already surrounded by several family members—all of whom I dreaded seeing.

My mother hugged Tiffany as Fred stood behind her with a wide, proud smile on his face. My father, Carmen, and Justine stood nearby, awaiting their turns. Tim, Tiffany's father, could be seen making his way through the crowd with his wife, Ashley. Now, Tim was a very handsome man—tall and slim and dark-skinned with huge facial features. He reminded me of Idris Elba sans the accent. When I was younger, I thought he was the most handsome man on earth.

Ashley was about my height and a little thinner than me. She was brown-skinned and wore her hair in burgundy and black micro-braids. She was usually pretty friendly and enough time had passed that I was over the fact that she happened to be the woman Tim left me for. Ashley had always been nice and kind to Tiffany, which was all I could ask of her.

Tim nodded in my direction as if a simple hello would just require too much effort from him. Ashley smiled and mouthed, "Hi." I returned her smile and then noticed Tim's mom, Nelda, standing behind Ashley. The smile quickly faded from my lips.

Wow, I thought, *she had the nerve to show up?*

I stood back and watched as, one by one, family member after family member hugged and congratulated Tiffany. Nelda was especially enthusiastic as she grabbed Tiffany and kissed her cheek.

"Grandma is so proud of you!" she gushed as she handed Tiffany an envelope.

"Thank you for coming," Tiffany said through a forced smile.

Tiffany hadn't been around Nelda that much. Actually, I don't think Nelda had spent more than five minutes with Tiffany throughout the entire eighteen years of her life. She'd just never taken much of an interest in her—probably because she never really liked me.

"Well, who's up for a steak dinner on me?" my father announced rather than asked.

"He knows I ain't going nowhere with him," my mother muttered under her breath. Fred tugged at her arm and she glared at him.

"What was that, Edna?" my father asked.

I sure hoped he wasn't challenging her because, though they'd been divorced for several years, my mother was always looking for a reason to cuss him out.

My mother snapped her head toward my father, but before she could respond, Tim said, "Well, Ashley and I were hoping that Tiff would come and celebrate with us at our house. Mama'll be there along with all of my sisters and their kids."

Before anyone else could speak, Tiffany held up her hand. "Um, actually, I was hoping to spend the evening with my mom. I'll be moving in a couple of days, so this is the only time we'll have together."

There was dead silence from the group. I looked around at the faces of my family members and ex-family members and stifled a smile. That was my girl—smart, level-headed, and not afraid to speak her mind. It was obvious that she'd shocked them all. My mother, however, was undoubtedly at least partially drunk and wasn't about to take no for an answer.

"Now look, I know—" she began, but was interrupted by Fred.

"Come on, Edna. Give her the gift so we can go have our 'happy hour.'" He tugged on the sleeve of her blouse as he turned toward the exit.

She frowned at him, and then I suppose the thought of having "happy hour" finally registered in her mind. She handed Tiffany an envelope, kissed her cheek, and then rolled her eyes at my father before following Fred out of the arena.

"Same old drunk Edna," my father scoffed.

I closed my eyes and shook my head.

Shortly thereafter, Tiffany and I headed to our favorite restaurant. That night, Tiffany made me proud in more ways than she could have ever known.

~*~

Around five the next morning, I was awakened by the ringing of my cell phone. At first, I thought I was dreaming. When I realized the phone was actually ringing, I turned over, switched on the lamp next to my bed, picked up the phone, and checked the screen. I recognized the number as Darius's. *What could he be calling for at this time of the morning?*

I frowned and then decided to let it roll to voicemail. If it was important, he'd leave a message. Then again, what could be important enough for him to be calling me at 5:00 A.M.? I shrugged and laid the phone back on the night table. I rested my head on my pillow and no sooner than I'd closed my eyes, my message alert sounded. I grabbed the phone and listened to the message which further puzzled me. The only thing I heard was several voices in the background but no actual message for me. I was just about to call Darius back when my phone rang again. It was him.

I answered with a soft, "Hello?" and waited for Darius's reply.

"Hello, Marli?" inquired the voice on the other end, a voice that definitely did not belong to Darius.

"Uh, yes. Who is this? Where's Darius?"

"This is Officer Garman with the Pine Bluff Police," he answered.

I sat up straight in the bed and felt my heart begin to race. What was a police officer doing with Darius's phone, and why was he calling *me*? Had Darius been arrested? Did the police think I was into drugs, too? I was so gripped with fear that I just held the phone and my chest. I couldn't speak.

"Ma'am, are you still there?"

"Um-uh-yes," I stammered. "W… why are you calling me? Where is Darius?"

"Um, ma'am, we're trying to locate his next of kin, and your text message to Mr. Cotton was the last communication received on his phone. You all were to have a meeting of some sort yesterday evening?"

"Um, well, he was gonna meet me at my daughter's graduation. Why do you need his next of kin?"

"Are you related to Mr. Cotton?"

"Well, no. We're friends. What's going on? Where is he?" Now I was really beginning to worry.

"Well, Ms.—"

I sighed. "*Meadows*."

"Ms. Meadows, Mr. Cotton's body was found near Lake Saracen about two hours ago."

"Body? Darius is…" My voice trailed off as the reality of what the officer had just told me began to sink in.

Darius was dead.

"Yes, ma'am. He was shot. We think the incident occurred around 7:00 P.M. last evening. Near the time you sent the message to him. We need to contact his next of kin."

I held the phone to my ear and tried to process the officer's words. Someone had shot Darius. They'd shot him and left him by the lake like he was nothing. He was gone and he wasn't coming back.

I felt a single tear trickle down my cheek. No, Darius wasn't the love of my life, but he was a human being, and no one deserved to be gunned down in cold blood.

"Ma'am, do you know any of his family members that we can notify of his death?"

"He... uh, he has a sister who lives here," I said, barely above a whisper. "Her name is Shondra. Shondra Coleman. Her number should be in his phone. All of his other relatives live out of town, I think."

"Okay, thank you, Ms. Meadows. We may be in touch later on."

"Okay."

I set my phone back on the night table and lay back down in my bed. As I rested my head on the pillow, I closed my eyes, said a prayer, and cried for Darius and his family. Before I knew it, I'd fallen into a troubled sleep.

FIVE

"IMMIGRANT"

I smiled brightly and waved as Tiffany walked through the security checkpoint alongside my father. He'd only bought two tickets to Atlanta and had made it abundantly clear that my presence was not needed. He'd help her move into her dorm and purchase everything she needed once they got there. To be honest, I didn't even want to go. I didn't feel like flying anywhere, and I didn't care to spend hours with my father.

I watched as they made their way to their gate, disappearing into the bustling crowd at the Bill and Hillary Clinton National Airport. I sighed. My only child was headed off to begin what promised to be a future filled with success, and I was headed back to the town I was born and raised in. Back to a job I didn't even like and to an empty house which had evolved from a gift to a prison.

As I made my way through the airport and out onto the short-term parking lot, I recalled the events of the last few weeks. Everything seemed to be changing around me while it felt like I was just standing still and watching it happen.

As I reached my car, unlocked the door, and climbed inside, it hit me. I *was* standing still. I was glued to the same spot, feeling the same feelings of disappointment I'd always felt. While everything around me was so dynamic, I'd become stagnant and complacent. I was perpetually unhappy.

I sat in my car and stared out the window at the hustle and bustle surrounding the airport. I watched as people stepped out of cars or cabs, bid farewell to loved ones, pulled their luggage behind them, and headed off to their individual destinations. I started my car and was halfway to the toll booth when I decided to stop and call Carla.

"Hello?" she answered after the first ring.

"Hey, it's Marli," I replied.

"Yeah, I know. What's up? I'm in the middle of packing."

"What do I need to do to sign up with Dana?"

"You're going to St. Louis with me?!" she asked, excitedly.

I smiled. "Yeah, I think I am."

~*~

I sat in the passenger's seat of Carla's Ford Expedition and inhaled her new cherry-scented air freshener. I was deep in thought about the events that had taken place over the previous week or so. Tiffany had flown off to Atlanta and had begun summer classes at Spelman. I'd attended Darius's wake, having decided to forego the funeral service. I'd submitted a leave of absence to the hospital, signed a three-month contract with Dana's staffing agency, locked up my house, and was on my way to St. Louis.

As Carla sped along Highway 67, I peered out the window, watching the other cars and wondering where their personal journeys would lead them. I wondered about my own journey, too. We were well into our six-hour trip and some of the anxiety I'd been experiencing had subsided, but I was still feeling the pangs of uncertainty that always seemed to accompany a new experience.

"You okay over there?" Carla asked, darting her eyes from the road to my face.

"Yeah, I'm all right. Just a little nervous, though," I replied, switching my gaze from the window to the radio. Some song I'd never heard before was playing, and it was beginning to annoy me.

"Well, you shouldn't be nervous. This is an adventure for you, *for us*. Besides, you definitely needed a change of pace, and I needed to get away from my own crazy life."

I looked over at Carla and smiled. Carla was a gorgeous woman with sepia skin that almost matched mine. She had small, expressive eyes and a small nose and mouth to match. She wore her hair in kinky twists and she had the figure of a sixteen-year-old. She wasn't rail thin, but I wouldn't consider her to be overweight, either. She was blessed with an hour-glass figure that I coveted.

Yet, even with her looks, she'd had no better luck in the love department than I had. She'd been married for eleven years but had been separated for the past several months. She'd caught her husband, Bryan, with another woman and had immediately thrown him out of the house. Their sons, Derek and Patrick, were spending the summer with their father while Carla worked in St. Louis. Carla was the strongest woman I knew. While my divorce had devastated me and nearly sent me into a full-fledged nervous breakdown, Carla hadn't missed a beat. She'd continued to work and take care of her sons without even seeming to give Bryan a second thought.

"I bet the boys were sad to see you go," I said as I pressed the button to scan the stations on her radio.

She smiled. "Well, Derek was pretty nonchalant about it. I guess since he's ten, he doesn't think he needs me anymore. But Patrick was pretty upset. But then again, Patrick's always been a mama's boy." That much I knew to be true. Patrick was seven and loved to stick near his mother.

"It must've been hard to leave them."

Carla sighed. "Honestly, Marli, I really needed the break. I love my boys, but it hasn't been easy doing all of this alone. I don't envy what you've been through. I figure that maybe I can make enough money this summer that I won't have to work in the fall. That way I can devote more time and attention to them."

I flashed her a concerned look. "You don't think you and Bryan will ever get back together?"

Carla shrugged. "I really don't know, Marli. I love Bryan, and I always will, but although I can forgive him, I know I'll never forget what he did. He cheated on me with a member of our church. I always trusted him, and now that trust is gone. What kind of marriage can we have if I can't trust him?"

"I don't know, Carla. I just hate for you and the kids to have to go through a divorce. Is Bryan still calling, begging to come home?"

Carla nodded. "Yeah, every other day and coming by the house with all kinds of lame excuses. I just need a break from all of it."

I nodded. "I can understand that."

"So did you tell your parents you were leaving?"

It was my turn to sigh. "Yeah, I told them. Of course they both thought I was crazy to leave my 'real' job and take off for some temporary assignment. I just listened to them. I wasn't in the mood to argue."

Carla smiled. "Well, I'm proud of you. There was a time when you never would've done this knowing they disapproved."

"Yeah, well, I'm quickly finding out there isn't much about me that they *do* approve of. So why try?"

"Well, I just try to live life the way I want to and make my own decisions. That way, when something goes wrong, I have no one to blame but myself."

"Good idea," I said and then stopped the radio on a smooth jazz station.

Carla shook her head. "There you go with that jazz. Dang, Marli! I don't see how you can listen to that stuff. Who is that singing anyway?"

I rolled my eyes. "It's Sade. Now you *know* I love me some Sade."

She shrugged. "It sounds all right, I guess."

"It sounds *excellent*. You really need to broaden your horizons. Talk about me being stuck in a rut. It wouldn't kill you to listen to someone other than Usher or Trey Songz, you know?"

Carla waved her hand in the air. "Okay, okay. I'll listen to Ms. Sade, but if I get sleepy and run off the road and kill us, it's on you."

I laughed. "You'll stay alert. Sade sings to your soul."

"Mm-hmm, well Usher and Trey Songz sing to my *everything else*."

I laughed again and relaxed against the seat. Maybe this trip *was* just what I needed. I was leaving my life behind—at least for the next three months. Maybe I could start a new one. Maybe I could become a new Marli.

SIX

"DIAMOND LIFE"

I stepped into the apartment that Carla and I would be sharing for the next three months and smiled. It was a modest, two-bedroom space with clean, beige carpets and pristine, white walls. It smelled of fresh paint and pine cleaner. It was completely furnished with sturdy—though not particularly aesthetic—furniture. The small living room included a navy blue sofa and arm chair, a set of oak end tables with a matching coffee table, and a metal TV stand, which was missing a TV.

"Wow, they couldn't include a TV?" Carla asked.

I shrugged. "I guess they don't consider a TV furniture."

I stepped into the kitchen to find that it was fully equipped—including a microwave oven. There was even a compact washer and dryer set.

"At least we won't have to go to the laundromat," I said.

Carla rolled her eyes. "Yay."

I sighed. "Carla, what did you expect? A penthouse?"

"No, just not *this*."

"Well, we can make it feel like home. I'm gonna go and pick out my bedroom."

"Yeah, sure. Doesn't matter to me," she muttered.

I shook my head and continued through the apartment. I checked out both bedrooms and settled on the smaller of the two since it included a window that overlooked the pool.

I took a seat on the bed and checked my phone. No missed calls. *Tiff must be staying pretty busy*, I thought. I hadn't heard from her in a couple of days, but I didn't want to bother her. I sat there for a moment and caught my breath. The next day would be my first day of work at St. Louis's University Hospital.

~*~

I stifled a yawn as I sat in one of the conference rooms within University Hospital. It was 8:00 A.M., I hadn't slept well in my new, temporary home, and I had the bags under my eyes to prove it. I brought a Styrofoam cup of stale coffee to my lips and took a sip, hoping it would jolt me out of my drowsy state. Next to me sat Carla, who'd evidently slept well and was wide awake.

The room was full of a variety of scrub-clad men and women,

some permanent employees and others temporary help like Carla and me. We were all waiting for the orientation session to begin.

The 356-bed hospital employed hundreds of healthcare professionals and, like many other facilities of its kind across the nation, it was experiencing a nursing shortage on top of a strike. Evidently, they were in need of other staff as well, which explained the presence of Carla and several other respiratory therapists and ancillary staff members.

Carla leaned over and whispered, "How you holding up, Marli? You gonna make it?"

I nodded. "Yeah, you know I specialize in functioning on minimal sleep."

"Yeah, me, too."

Our conversation was halted by a loud voice coming from the front of the room. Speaking was a petite woman who wore a bright smile and a stark white shirt. An ID badge hung from the left side of the shirt's stiff collar.

"Good morning. I know all of you are anxious to get started and to be dismissed. I'm April Hence, the training coordinator here at the hospital, and I wanna first thank you for choosing to work here at University Hospital, and I also wanna extend a warm welcome on behalf of the CEO," she said. And with that, orientation began.

Three hours later, we were handed our floor assignments.

Carla nudged me. "Ha! ICU! I'm so happy."

Carla had always loved working in the critical care areas of the hospital. She was a true adrenaline junkie. I really didn't care where I worked.

"Well, good for you." I unfolded my own slip of paper. "ER," I read aloud.

I wasn't surprised about the assignment. I'd worked in so many areas at the hospital back home, I figured they'd want me in a critical area.

"Wow, that should be interesting. This is like *the* trauma hospital for this area," Carla said.

I nodded. "Yeah, shouldn't be a dull moment, huh?"

After we were dismissed, we went to check out our work areas and meet our new supervisors. Then we went home to rest up. Both Carla and I were scheduled to begin working our regular shifts the following evening at 7:00 P.M.

SEVEN

"SMOOTH OPERATOR"

We'd been living and working in St. Louis for exactly three weeks. Well, truthfully, I use the term "living" loosely, because all we'd really been doing was working, eating, and sleeping. After twelve hours in the ER, it was all I could do to drag myself to Carla's car in the morning and then into my bed once we made it home. In those three, short weeks, I'd seen several stabbing and gunshot victims, a few guys who'd ended up on the wrong end of a fist fight, more than my fair share of motor vehicle accident injuries, and several cases that were more than suitable for an episode of Untold Stories of the ER. I was emotionally drained and physically exhausted, so when Carla brought up the idea of us going out for drinks, I jumped at the chance.

She'd heard about Charmaine's, a popular "grown and sexy" club located downtown, and we'd made plans to meet up there with a couple of ladies who also worked at the hospital. So, with me dressed in a silver, off-the-shoulder blouse and black slacks, and Carla in a tight, red dress and black stilettos, we headed out for an evening of relaxation and fun.

As Carla pulled out of our building's parking lot, I checked my cell phone and saw that I'd missed a call from Tiffany. I decided to call her in the morning and tucked my phone away as I took in the images of St. Louis nightlife that flashed through the window.

Ten minutes later, we arrived at Charmaine's. I smiled as we entered the club. It was small and cozy and filled with round tables covered with black table cloths and accented with centerpieces of vibrant, red roses. The dim lighting added a sense of intimacy to the place.

It didn't take long for us to find the two ladies we were meeting. Carolyn and Ronda waved at us from their seats right in front of the small stage. I was happy that they'd managed to get us a good table.

The ladies greeted us with bright smiles and a promise that the band slated to perform that night, The St. Louis Kingsmen, would be good. I took a seat, ordered a strawberry daiquiri, and anxiously awaited the show while chatting with the ladies. Thankfully, we didn't have to wait long at all.

"Welcome to Charmaine's, everyone!" proclaimed the short, stocky man with a booming voice, seizing our undivided attention.

The crowd applauded in response. I looked across the table and smiled at Carla. I couldn't remember the last time I'd been out and it felt *great*.

"Thank you for coming out tonight. You will not be disappointed," the announcer continued. "Back by popular demand, we give you, *all* The St. Louis Kingsmen!"

He left the stage and the lights brightened to reveal the full band—a drummer, keyboardist, two guitarists, a saxophonist, and a trumpeter. I took a sip of my daiquiri and clasped my hands before me on the table as they began to play a mid-tempo song. It was one of my favorite Sweetback tunes.

They were good, *very good*. I leaned over to share the sentiment with Carolyn.

"I told you they were good. We heard them a couple of weeks ago. The lead singer is *awesome*," she said.

I nodded and returned my attention to the stage where the lead singer was now approaching the microphone as he continued to strum his guitar. His voice was smooth and rich and the music they provided was nothing short of aural beauty. I swayed and snapped my fingers and thoroughly enjoyed myself. They played a satisfying mix of smooth jazz and R&B and, by the time they took their break, I didn't think I could take anymore, but the second half of the show proved to be even better than the first.

Through the second half of the show, I found it hard to take my eyes off of the lead singer. He was tall, dark, sexy, and *very* handsome, and his voice had me absolutely mesmerized. He sang with so much emotion and soul. I sat there and watched him perform and wondered if he smelled as good as he looked. I was really feeling him.

I leaned over to Carolyn again and asked, "Who *is* that guy?"

"Who, the lead singer?"

I nodded but didn't take my eyes off of him. I could've sworn he was looking at me, too.

"Quinton Farver. Gorgeous, isn't he? Women come from miles around to see him perform. He's gonna be a big star one day."

"Yeah," I agreed and then continued to enjoy the show.

The last song was an instrumental tune that featured solos from each individual musician. I was especially impressed by the trumpeter, who was the only non-African American in the band. He was a tall, white guy with short, dark-blond hair. He played that trumpet like he was full of the soul of a black man.

After two encores, the show ended with a standing ovation from the entire crowd. Carla and I decided to stay a little while longer, both of us hating to see the evening come to an end. We'd really enjoyed this night out with Carolyn and Ronda and were discussing plans for our next weekend off when a waitress approached me.

She placed a fresh daiquiri in front of me. "Here you are, ma'am."

"Oh, wait," I said, stopping her in her tracks as she turned to leave. "I didn't order another."

She gave me a knowing smile. "Complements of Mr. King."

I frowned. I didn't know any Mr. King. "Um, who is Mr. King?"

"A member of the band," she replied and then walked away.

I sat there with a confused look on my face as the other ladies at the table broke into a refrain of "oh's" and "ah's," along with verbal speculations as to who Mr. King could've been. After much deliberation, the consensus was that Mr. King was probably the keyboardist since Carla claimed to have seen him looking at our table more than once. I had no idea who Mr. King was, but I did want to thank him for the drink. I decided that if he *was* the keyboardist, it wouldn't exactly be a bad thing. He wasn't as handsome as Quinton, but he was cute.

The other ladies continued to chatter on. I continued to sip my drink and was shocked to see the trumpeter from the band approaching our table a few minutes later. *Maybe he's relaying a message from the keyboardist*, I thought. He pulled a chair from the table next to ours and sat down beside me.

"You enjoying your drink?" he asked. I was taken aback by the fact that he sounded like a black man.

"Um, yes, I am," I answered.

He smiled, revealing two rows of perfectly white teeth. His blue eyes sparkled as he spoke. "Good, I thought you might want another one."

I nearly choked. "You mean *you* bought this drink for me?"

He nodded. "Yeah. And I'd like to buy you dinner one day, too."

I looked around at my table mates and smiled. Were they pulling a fast one on me?

"Oh no, is this a joke?" I asked.

His brow furrowed. "No, why?"

"Well, I haven't ever been approached by a guy like you before," I replied, choosing my words carefully.

"What? A trumpet player? Don't tell me you've got something against dating musicians," he said with a serious look on his face.

Damn, I'm gonna have to just come on out and say it. "No, I mean a… a *white guy*. I've only ever dated black men, you know?"

He leaned closer to me. "Oh, so you have something against dating white men?"

I leaned back and frowned. "Well… no, that's not what I'm saying. I mean, I've just never dated outside of my race before. That's all."

He raised his eyebrows. "Really? Well, I've never dated inside mine."

I tilted my head to the side. "Really? Never?"

"Really. *Never.* So, what's your name? Mine's Chris. Chris King," he said and then gave me a lopsided grin.

I returned his smile without even realizing it. "Um, it's Marli."

"Marley. Like Bob Marley?"

I nodded. "Yeah, but it's actually short for Marlena."

"Oh, that's cool, like the actress."

"Yeah, but spelled differently."

"I like it. So about that dinner..." Boy, was he persistent. He seemed nice enough and he was cute, but I just couldn't see myself dating him. I had a thing for brown skin and huge features, neither of which he possessed.

"Look, Chris. Thanks for the drink, but—"

He held up his hand, "But you don't date white men. Okay, okay. I get it. Well, enjoy the rest of your drink and the rest of your evening, Ms. Marli," he said, then stood to leave. He leaned over and whispered, "By the way, you have no idea what you're missing."

He looked me in the eye, flashed that smile at me again, and then left the table. As I watched him walk away, I couldn't help but notice that he had a pretty nice body and he oozed confidence.

"Wow, Marli," Carolyn said. "I didn't see that coming."

"Me, either," I replied, never taking my eyes off of Chris King.

"He seemed nice, though, and he has a certain swagger about him. You know what I mean?" Carolyn added.

"Yeah, he does."

I finally took my eyes off of him and looked across the table to find Carla engaged in a lively conversation with none other than Quinton Farver. Well, that figured.

EIGHT

"FLOW"

I arrived at work with only seconds to spare. Carla had decided at the last minute to call in sick. So, of course, she wasn't in any particular hurry to get me to the hospital on time. This situation really made me regret not bringing my own vehicle to St. Louis. Anyhow, while she was back at the apartment with a queasy stomach, I was poised for another exciting night in the ER. What would I walk into this shift?

No sooner than I'd swiped my badge and entered the trauma unit, I was herded into a room and instructed by the attending physician to begin chest compressions on a patient whom I knew nothing about. As I, along with another nurse, performed CPR on the elderly woman, I could see an elderly man standing outside the room with a concerned look on his face.

"What's going on here?" I asked the other nurse, Kerry, who was bagging the patient.

"Husband found her unconscious, lying in the backyard at their home. By the time EMS got her here, she was breathing but had a weak pulse. She's in full cardiac arrest now," she said as she squeezed the Ambu bag, allowing the oxygenated air to enter the patient's lungs.

I nodded and continued with the chest compressions. There were several other nurses in the room as well as Dr. Freeman, the attending physician. Behind me, I could hear him barking orders for different drugs to be pushed—atropine, epinephrine, lidocaine. All the while, we took quick breaks to check for a shockable heart rhythm. After thirty minutes of a valiant effort by all involved, the patient was pronounced deceased.

I watched as Dr. Freeman informed the patient's husband. The man's face fell and he hung his head in despair as he listened to the doctor. Then he silently walked away from the emergency area.

My heart ached for the man and, as we prepared the body for transport to the morgue, I silently prayed for him and his family. I hated to think of anyone losing a loved one.

And so began my shift. As usual, the twelve hours seemed to zip by, and by 7:00 A.M., I was more than ready to get home and into bed. My feet were throbbing, and I was truly exhausted. One thing was for sure, if I had never done so in the past, I was *definitely* earning my paycheck at University Hospital.

I gave my report on the patients that remained in the ER and then stepped outside into the warm June weather and took a seat on a bench. I expected Carla to be there any minute to pick me up, so I didn't mind waiting outside. I'd been sitting there a few minutes before I realized that I was sitting next to the elderly gentlemen who'd lost his wife the previous night. Had he stayed at the hospital all night?

"Sir," I began. "Sir, are you okay?"

He looked up at me with the saddest expression. "No, I… I lost my wife last night."

I nodded. "I know, sir. I'm very sorry for your loss."

He hung his head. "Thank you. Millie and I were together for fifty-four years. I don't know what I'm gonna do now. There's a piece of me that's gone forever."

I looked down at the sidewalk for a moment, not exactly sure of what to say. Finally, I said, "Have you been here all night?"

He nodded. "I can't go home. I can't go home knowing Millie's not there." His voice broke.

I placed my hand on his shoulder. "Do you have any family you could stay with for a while? Is there anyone I could call for you?"

He wiped his eyes. "Um, we've got a daughter, Sarah. She lives across town. I've been so upset, I haven't been able to call her."

I offered him a smile. "Okay, let me call her for you."

The man gave me his name and his daughter's number. I called and informed her that her father was at the ER and needed a ride home. I decided to let him be the one to break the news about her mother to her. I sat with him and helped him to his daughter's car once she arrived. It was as they drove away that I realized Carla still hadn't arrived to pick me up. It had been exactly thirty minutes since my shift ended when I dialed her cell phone number—no answer. I left a message and continued to wait on the bench.

Another twenty minutes passed and I could barely keep my eyes open as I fumbled through my purse for my phone, having decided to try and call Carla again. I'd finally fished my phone out of my purse when I was startled by a voice coming from the driveway in front of the ER.

"Well, if it isn't Ms. Marli," a man said. I raised my head to see that it was Chris King.

He was speaking to me from the driver's side of a shiny, black Mercedes Benz, complete with some very expensive-looking chrome rims. Trumpet-playing must have been a lucrative career for him.

"Hi," I said unenthusiastically.

"You work here?"

Well that was stating the obvious. I was sitting outside a hospital wearing scrubs.

"Uh, yeah. Just got off," I said, rather curtly.

"Oh, okay, well, have a good day." I'm sure he sensed that I wasn't in the best of moods.

"Yeah, it's been lovely so far," I replied under my breath.

He drove away, and I dialed Carla's number again. This time it went straight to voicemail. A voice inside told me that I should've asked Mr. Chris King for a ride, but I didn't really know him. What if he was some kind of psycho?

After another ten minutes of waiting, I looked up and noticed a familiar black Mercedes pull back around the driveway.

"Do you just like hanging around hospitals or something, or are you a stalker?" I asked sarcastically as he pulled his car to a stop in front of me.

Chris smiled and shook his head. "No and no. I was here dropping off my sister for her shift. She's a nurse. Her name's Ava King. You know her?"

I shook my head. "No, but I'm new here." *And I don't know many white people, period.*

"Oh, okay. Well, anyway, after I drove off earlier, I thought to myself that you looked like you needed a ride home. Do you?"

"I'm okay. I'm sure my friend will be here any minute," I said and glanced at my watch. Now, of course I was lying, because at that point, I wasn't sure if Carla was *ever* going to show up.

"You sure? How long you been out here waiting?"

I cleared my throat. "About an hour."

"Man, that's a long time, and you look tired. Come on, I'll give you a ride."

I frowned. "I don't know. Maybe I'll just catch a cab…"

"Come on, Ms. Marli. Why you gotta be so mean? I'm trying to help you, here. You got something against riding in cars with white men, too?"

I sighed, grabbed my bag, and walked over to his car. At that point I was so tired, I couldn't even argue anymore.

Chris jumped out of the car and opened the passenger's door for me. Even through drowsy eyes I couldn't help but notice how nicely his jeans fit him. And he smelled *so good*.

Once I climbed inside, he closed the door behind me and returned to the driver's seat. His car's interior was immaculate. The heavenly aroma of a vanilla-scented air freshener filled my nose and Marcus Miller's "Boomerang" was pouring softly from the car's speakers.

As we exited the lot, I looked over at him and smiled. "Thanks," I said.

He glanced at me with a grin. "No problem, Ms. Marli. Where to?"

I gave him my address and said, "Can I ask you a question?"

"Yeah, what's up?"

"Why do you talk like that?"

He gave me a confused look. "Like what?"

"You know, like you're black."

His eyes widened. "Oh... uh, this is how I've always talked."

"Really?"

"Yeah, really. Why?"

I shrugged. "I was just wondering."

Chris shook his head. "Wow, you *are* prejudiced. Where are you from, anyway? Selma circa 1954?"

I rolled my eyes. "I'm not prejudiced. I was just curious. And I'm from Arkansas."

"Oh damn, no wonder. They probably still got segregated schools and 'whites only' restaurants down there," he said with an exaggerated Southern drawl.

I bugged my eyes. "No, they don't!"

"Well, that's how you're acting. If I didn't know any better, I'd think you were from the Jim Crow era instead of Arkansas."

I rolled my eyes. "Whatever."

"I'm serious. I don't think I've ever met a woman as racist as you before."

"I'm not racist!"

"If you say so…"

A silence fell between us for the remainder of the ride. And all the while, only one thought ran through my mind: *Am I being racist?*

As we approached my building, I said, "Well… thanks again. I really appreciate the ride." I paused for a moment. "Look, I really didn't mean anything by asking that question. I wasn't trying to be a racist or anything, seriously."

He smiled. "I know. I was just messing with you." He jumped out of the car and opened the door for me. "I'll walk you to your door."

"Okay, but you don't have to."

He shot me a sly look. "Maybe I want to."

As Chris walked me to my apartment, the urge to twist my hips was overwhelming. As tired as I was, I still found it almost impossible not to flirt with him.

Once we reached my door, I gave him a groggy smile. "Um, well, this is it. I'd invite you in, but I'm so tired, it'll be all I can do to climb into my bed."

Chris nodded. "No problem, I got you. But you know, there *is* a way you could repay me."

I tilted my head to the side. "Really? And what's that?"

He raised his eyebrows. "Dinner?"

I sighed and shook my head. "Look Chris, like I said before, I don't date white guys." But I was kind of thinking about it at that point.

"I know, but you said yourself that I don't sound white. You could just close your eyes and pretend that I'm black."

I had to laugh at that. "I don't think I can eat dinner with my eyes closed, Mr. King, or do you plan on feeding me?"

"I will if I have to. Come on, Ms. Marli. One dinner, no strings attached. That's all I'm asking."

I looked up at his face and smiled. He did have the nicest blue eyes. "Why?"

"Why what?" he asked, looking confused again.

"Why are you so interested in having dinner with me?"

"Oh, well, when I saw you at the club, I thought, *Dang, now that's a beautiful woman.* Do you know how hard it was for me to concentrate on playing my horn with you sitting there looking like you were looking? I just wanna spend a little time in the presence of your beauty and get to know you. Plus, you're mean, and I like that in a woman."

Despite myself, I felt my smile widening. "Okay, I'll think about it. What's your phone number?"

I programmed Chris's number into my phone and then knocked

on the door. I guess I was too tired to remember that I had the key in my purse. Chris and I were both shocked when Quinton Farver opened the door, wearing only a pair of boxers.

"Uh," was all I managed to say.

Chris, however, was more verbal. "Quint? What you doing here?"

"Aw, just kickin' it with my girl, Carla. You must be Marli. I was just getting ready to leave," he said.

I frowned a little. "Uh, yeah. Nice to meet you?"

He moved to the side and, as I squeezed past him, I turned and said, "Thanks again, Chris."

"No problem, Ms. Marli. I'll be waiting for your call."

I nodded and continued through the apartment to my room. I closed the door, stripped out of my work clothes, and collapsed into the bed. I decided to confront Carla about her little fake illness whenever I woke up.

~*~

I rolled over in bed and silenced the alarm on my cell phone. 3:00 P.M. already? It was time for me to drag myself out of bed, find something to eat, and get ready to head back to the hospital for another shift. I'd been asleep ever since I arrived home and had yet to confront Carla about her undercover booty call. Oh, and I couldn't forget the fact that she left me high and dry without a ride home that morning. It wasn't like Carla to be irresponsible, and her behavior really concerned me.

After a hot shower, I wrapped my robe around my body and headed to the kitchen, hoping that Carla was awake so that I could talk to her. I walked into the kitchen and was surprised to find her at the stove whipping up something that smelled so good, I could've sworn I'd stepped into a restaurant.

"Hey, sleepy head," she greeted me cheerfully with a bright smile. I guess her time with Quinton had energized her.

"Hey," I said brusquely as I took a seat at the table. Whatever she was cooking was not going to make up for the fact that she'd left me in the lurch for a piece of tail.

Carla sighed and took a seat across from me. "Look, Marli... I'm sorry about this morning. The time just got away from me."

"Mm-hmm. I imagine it did, Carla."

"I'm trying to apologize. You gonna cut me some slack here?"

With a furrowed brow, I said, "Let's see here. You lied about being sick so that you could play bedroom gymnastics with some guy you barely know, and then you just left me sitting outside the ER like some orphan. I had to catch a ride with that Justin

Timberfake from the club. He could've been a serial killer or something! What kind of best friend are you?!"

Carla shook her head. "Naw, that white dude is way too fine to be a serial killer. A man can't be that fine and be a psycho at the same time. It's against the laws of nature."

I rolled my eyes. "What is wrong with you? When did you start lying? Why would you leave me hanging like that?"

Carla dropped her head. "Look, I didn't tell you about Quinton because I knew you'd judge me."

"Judge you? Carla, you're still married! I'm not judging you. I'm just concerned."

"Yeah, well I don't feel married anymore."

"Yeah, but you *are* married, and what about your kids?"

"I talk to my boys every day. They're fine. Bryan's always been a good father. They're in good hands."

"I know that, but you need to get yourself together. You can't just be sleeping with random guys, Carla. That's dangerous."

Carla shook her head. "I know what I'm doing, Marli. Just like you knew what you were doing with Darius."

My eyes widened. "Wow, that was a low blow, Carla."

She leaned back and crossed her arms over her chest. "Well, you took it there. Anyway, who are you to judge me? I remember all those guys you hooked up with after your divorce."

Dang, that stung. "You're right, Carla. I did hook up with a bunch of guys, but I never pretended that what I was doing was right. I was hurt and mixed up in the head. And besides, the operative word is *divorced*. I was not married when I did that stuff."

Without blinking an eye, she said, "I'm divorced in my heart."

I shook my head. "Okay, I see that this conversation is going nowhere. I'm done talking about this, Carla. But you better be careful. You make a practice of calling in, and you're gonna lose this gig."

"*Look*, it was the only time Quinton had free to spend with me. And believe me, he was *more* than worth it!"

I looked up to heaven. "Lord, help her…"

She leaned forward. "No, really. He was *grrreat*! You should try him. I don't mind, really."

Was she for real? "No thanks, I'll pass."

She shrugged. "Your loss. Anyway, I'm sorry about not picking you up. Next time you can just take my truck."

"Next time? Really, Carla? *Whatever*." I stood to leave the kitchen.

"Wait!" she called after me. "Don't you want something to eat?

I'm fixing chicken cacciatore."

Chicken cacciatore was my favorite, and she knew it, but I wasn't about to break bread with her. "No. I think I just lost my appetite," I said. "Oh, and I'm going to church with Carolyn and Ronda on Sunday. You *might* wanna join us."

NINE

"SKIN"

I woke up on Sunday morning with a smile. I hadn't been to church since before we left Arkansas, and Lord knows with all I'd witnessed in the ER, I needed some spiritual food. I stretched and yawned and headed to my closet where I chose a black pencil skirt, gold blouse, and gold pumps. I showered, slipped on my robe, and headed to the kitchen for a quick breakfast. I was surprised to see Carla already at the table.

"Good morning," she said. "You're up early for an off day."

I opened the refrigerator door and peered inside. "Yeah, I'm going to church, remember?"

"Oh, yeah. You did say something about that the other day."

I fixed myself a bagel with cream cheese, a few grapes and strawberries, and took a seat at the table across from Carla.

"Um, so, does the offer still stand?" she asked.

"What offer?"

"To go to church with you guys."

I looked up at her. "Of course it does. Carolyn's picking me up around 10:30."

Carla smiled. "Okay, let me go and get ready. Um, which church is it?"

I shrugged. "I honestly can't remember the name. Carolyn was invited by a girl who works on the oncology unit. I think her father's the pastor or something. Anyway, she and Ronda went a couple of weeks ago and she said the service was awesome."

"Well, I hope so. I could use some awesome worship right about now."

I nodded and watched as she headed out of the kitchen. *We could all use that*, I thought.

~*~

The four of us filed into the Spirit and Truth Worship Center just minutes before service began. It was a huge church and the sanctuary was full of people. We sat near the back, and I took the few moments to glance through the church bulletin. On the cover was a picture of a handsome, older African American couple—the pastor and his wife.

As music began to fill the sanctuary, many members of the congregation sprang to their feet and clapped their hands. I ended up having to stand, myself, just to get a good view of the choir. I made a mental note to be sure and get there early next time so I could get a good seat.

I closed my eyes and swayed and clapped to the rhythm of the music. It felt *so good* to be in church, and that choir could definitely sing! As the lead singer began singing the first verse of Hezekiah Walker's "I'll Make It," I opened my eyes to get a glimpse of him. I nearly fell over when I saw the man with the smooth voice clutching the microphone, singing his heart out.

No, it can't be him, I thought. *Maybe I'm just too far back to be sure, but that sure does look like—*

Carla nudged me and whispered, "Hey, isn't that the white guy from that jazz band up there singing? You know, your Justin Timberfake?"

"It looks like him, but it *can't* be," I replied without taking my eyes off of him.

But truthfully, he had the same mannerisms as Chris, and by the end of the song, I was just about certain that it *was* him. What was he doing in a black church singing like a black man and looking really nice at the same time? He was dressed in a black suit and pink shirt with a black tie, and he sure wore it well.

The choir finished the song and I took my seat and watched as

Chris King walked over to the music pit. I wondered just what he was really all about. I had to admit to myself that there was definitely something intriguing about him and, well, that I was kind of attracted to him. He was tall and handsome and just plain *fine*, but I still couldn't see myself dating him. It just seemed too weird.

The service flowed smoothly, but it was a contrast to the services I was accustomed to. This was a non-denominational church, and several elements of Baptist worship were missing. It was definitely a different experience for me, but I liked it. The sermon was a powerful mixture of preaching and teaching, and the pastor was full of fire!

After the service ended, I quickly made my way to the front to speak to Chris and found myself at the rear of a crowd of his admirers. Evidently, several of the women at the church had set their sights on Mr. Chris King, and I can honestly say that I understood why. He seemed like quite a catch.

I stood there and waited for a few moments before deciding to leave. I hated to keep my friends waiting. I had just made it back to where Carolyn, Ronda, and Carla were waiting for me when I felt a tap on my shoulder. Startled, I spun around to see that it was Chris.

"Ms. Marli! I thought that was you," he said with a bright smile.

I couldn't help but to smile back. "Yeah, I just wanted to tell you how much I enjoyed service, but you were occupied back there. You have a great voice."

"Thanks. I really appreciate that. That song is a little above my octave range, though."

I shook my head. "No, you were perfect."

"Well, thanks again."

We stood there in awkward silence for a moment and since I didn't have the good sense to do it, my friends introduced themselves to him.

Chris smiled and shook their hands. "I'm Chris King. Nice to meet you all." He turned to me and asked, "Um, have you thought anymore about that date?"

I adjusted my purse on my shoulder. "Um, well…"

"Well, if you're game, you can take me up on that offer right now," he continued.

I glanced at Carla and the other ladies. "Well, Chris, I kinda made plans already."

"No, no. You can eat dinner with us *anytime*," Carla said with a sly smile.

"Yes, you two go *right ahead*," Ronda interjected.

"Um, uh…" I stammered. Were they trying to set me up?

"Well, Ms. Marli. What do you say?"

"Um… okay, I guess," I finally answered with a shrug. What else was I supposed to say?

I said my goodbyes to my companions and followed Chris out to his vehicle.

"Where are we gonna eat?" I asked as he drove through a neighborhood of well-kept homes with neat lawns.

He glanced at me and smiled. "The best place in town."

"Oh, okay. What do they serve?"

"Soul food."

I laughed. "Soul food?"

"Yeah, soul food. You don't like soul food?"

I raised my eyebrows and looked over at him. "So because I'm black I gotta like soul food?"

He flashed me a serious look. "Why you gotta go there? Is everything about race with you? I just thought you'd like the food, that's all."

I dropped my eyes, feeling a little embarrassed. "I'm sorry. It was a joke, really."

"Well, would you rather we ate something else?" he asked, still sounding serious.

I shook my head and quietly said, "No, it's okay."

"You sure? I don't want you thinking that I'm trying to stereotype you or racially profile you or something."

I sighed. "I said it's fine, and I really am sorry."

He smiled. "Okay, we're here then."

He pulled the car onto the driveway in front of a neat, two-story house only a few blocks from the church.

"This is a restaurant?" I asked as he opened the car door for me.

"Nope, it's my parents' house."

My eyes widened as I looked up at his face. "Your *parents'* house?! You want me to meet your *parents*? Chris, you don't even *know* me." This might sound bad, but the thought of sitting at a table full of white people eating dinner really did not appeal to me.

"I'm *tryna* get to know you… if you'll let me. By the way, what's your last name?"

"See, this is crazy. You don't even know my last name!" I whispered as we approached the front door.

He raised his eyebrows. "That's why I'm asking. What is it?"

I shook my head. "Meadows. It's Marli Meadows."

"Okay, *dang*. Was that so hard, woman?" he said as if I was being absurd.

I rolled my eyes. "How do you know they'll even want to meet me?"

"Because I know my own parents. Stop being so uptight."

I had just about decided at that point to turn around and leave. I could've called Carla for a ride or even called for a cab. Nevertheless, I stayed. Maybe I wanted to see his parents' reaction to me. But then again, if he'd really never dated inside his race, there might not have been any reaction at all. For whatever reason, I didn't leave Chris's side, and I didn't resist when he grabbed my hand and held onto it.

Chris rang the doorbell and we stood there for what seemed like hours before a familiar-looking black woman finally answered the door. *Wow, they have a maid*, I thought. *No wonder he can afford that Mercedes.*

A huge smile spread across her face as she reached up and hugged Chris. "Chris! I didn't know you were coming for dinner. Thought you'd be headed back out of town with the band."

"Naw, we don't leave until the middle of next week. Besides, you know I wasn't gonna miss Sunday dinner at home," he replied as he planted a kiss on her cheek. Then he turned to me. "Marli, this is my mama, Elizabeth King. Mama, this is Marli Meadows. She's new to St. Louis."

I know I must've been looking crazy as I mechanically shook Mrs. King's hand. This woman was Chris's mother? It *couldn't* be. Chris was not mixed. He was very obviously white. Wasn't he?

"Hi," I said weakly.

"Nice to meet you, Marli," she said warmly and then returned her attention to Chris. "Chris, your father's in the living room. Dinner's not quite ready yet."

He kissed her on the cheek again. "Yes, ma'am."

Chris held my hand as he led me through the foyer and into the modestly decorated living room. The house was filled with the aroma of something truly heavenly. I couldn't readily identify what was cooking, but it definitely smelled good.

When we reached the living room and I saw Mr. King sitting in a recliner, I realized why Mrs. King had looked so familiar. I'd seen their faces on the front of the church bulletin. Mr.—or should I say *Reverend*—and Mrs. King were the pastor and first lady of the church.

"Old man, how'd y'all get here so quick?" Chris quipped as he approached his father.

Rev. King stood from his chair and embraced Chris. "Chris! I wasn't expecting you." He smiled at me. "Who we got here?"

"Dad, this is Marli. She's new in town. I told her this is the best place to eat in St. Louis."

Rev. King shook my hand. "Well, you won't be disappointed. My Lizzie can sure enough cook."

I smiled. "Thanks for having me."

"No problem. Any friend of Chris's is welcome here. He's my special boy, you know," he said as he looked proudly up at Chris, who stood a couple of inches taller than his father.

I smiled and took a seat on the sofa. Chris sat next to me and engaged his father in warm conversation as we waited for dinner. I could tell that they really shared a special bond.

I glanced around the room and eyed the photographs that decorated the various tables as well as the top of a piano. There were a few family portraits which included Rev. and Mrs. King, Chris and three young ladies. Chris was the only white person in any of the photos. There were pictures of him and the girls as children, teenagers, all the way up to adulthood.

This really was his family, and I was itching to know how it all came to be, but I dared not ask him and sound even more race-obsessed than he already thought I was. I turned my attention back to his and his father's conversation and tried to push the questions out of my head.

"So Marli, how long have you been here in town?" Rev. King asked.

"Um, a little over a month," I replied.

"Marli's a nurse, like Ava," Chris offered.

"Really? You working over at University, too?" Rev. King

queried.

"Um, yes, sir. I'm on a three-month assignment there. I'm from Arkansas."

"Arkansas. Got some relatives in Arkansas. Never can remember the name of the town, though. How's your stay here been so far?"

"Good. I like it here."

"Good, then maybe you'll decide to stay," Chris said with a wide grin.

TEN

"I NEVER THOUGHT I'D SEE THE DAY"

Dinner was nice, *really* nice. Mrs. King lived up to her reputation, and I thoroughly enjoyed her chicken and dressing, green beans, and homemade macaroni and cheese. After dinner, two of Chris's sisters, Ava and Lana, showed up and shared chocolate pie with us. They were both beautiful, short, and round, just like their mother.

During my visit, I learned that Chris was the oldest child and that Ava was the baby. Ava, of course, was a nurse, and Lana was a teacher. A third sister, Jayne, lived in Chicago and was a pastor's wife and stay-at-home mom.

Being there with them felt nice. They were a very close-knit family, and the love they shared was infectious. Chris was the adored big-brother, and he took his role as the protector of his sisters very seriously. He was both comfortable with and accepted by his family, two things that were never true of me and my family.

We'd been at his parents' house for hours, and I really wouldn't have minded staying longer, but right before nightfall, Chris decided to take me home. As we rode along in his Mercedes, I peered out the side window with a faint smile on my face.

"Did you enjoy yourself?" he asked.

I turned to him and nodded. "Yeah, I did. Your family is wonderful. You're very lucky."

"I am," he agreed. "I thank God for them every day."

"You should."

A few minutes later, Chris parked his car on the lot in front of my building. He turned to me and smiled. "So, when are you gonna ask me why I'm a white man with a black family?"

I shook my head. "I wasn't gonna ask."

"Really? You're not curious at all?"

"I didn't say I wasn't curious. I just figured if you wanted me to know, you'd tell me sooner or later."

He raised his eyebrows. "So you plan on there being a later for us, huh?"

I shrugged. "Maybe. Anything's possible."

"It sure is." He paused. "Okay, so my mama, Mrs. King, was really good friends with my biological mother; they grew up together. They were more like sisters, really. When she and my father, Rev. King, were newlyweds, they would babysit me all of the time. Mama didn't know until after my biological parents died in a car accident that they'd put it in their will for her and my dad to raise me if anything happened to them, since neither of them had any family left. I was only a year old when they died. I've been a King ever since."

"Wow, so they adopted you, officially?"

He nodded. "Yeah, but they let me keep my original last name, Russell. When I turned twelve, I told them I wanted it changed. That's when I became a King."

"That's beautiful, Chris. It's plain to see how loved you are. Your parents are some good people."

"Yeah, they sure are."

"Was it odd, you know, being the only white person in a black family?"

He shook his head. "Not at all. I don't even remember my biological parents. This is the only family I've ever known, and my parents never treated me any different than they did my sisters. I was praised when I did good and punished when I misbehaved just like Lana, Ava, and Jayne. I didn't even realize there was anything different about me until I got a lot older, like seven or eight."

"Really? What happened then?"

"Some kids at school teased me about my family being black and me being white, called me some weird names. I ran home and told my mama what they said and she explained to me that I was different, but that there was nothing wrong with me. I never forgot that."

"Well, you *are* different, but in a good way."

He cocked his head to the side. "Aw, thanks, Ms. Marli. I'm glad you think so."

We sat there in silence for a few moments and then I said, "Well, I guess I'd better be heading on up there." I gestured toward the apartment building.

Chris smiled. "Yeah, let me walk you."

"I can take care of myself, you know? I don't have to have an escort."

"Aw, now. I'm just getting to know you. I can't let anything happen to you."

He grabbed my hand and we walked silently through the building to my floor. Once we reached my door, he leaned over and kissed me softly on the cheek.

"Thanks for having dinner with me and my family, Ms. Marli," he whispered.

His breath felt warm against my ear, and the warmth seemed to travel down my body. I looked up at his face and smiled. For some reason he seemed to grow more and more handsome as the hours passed.

"No. Thank *you*. I really enjoyed it," I said softly.

He stood close to me and looked me in the eye. "Um, Marli? You think maybe I've earned a little favor from you?"

My gaze was fixed on his blue eyes. "Earned?"

He leaned in closer to me. "Yeah. Well, I *did* rescue you the other day when you were stranded at the hospital, right?"

I nodded. "That's right."

"And I dazzled you with my voice in church today..."

"Mm-hmm."

"And you've already met almost my entire family."

"That's true."

"So, you think maybe you could give me your number?"

"My number?"

He nodded and clasped his hands together. "Pretty please?"

I tried not to smile. "Well, what if I told you I already have a man and that he's back home waiting for me and he doesn't like me giving my phone number out to other guys?"

"Then I'd say that what he doesn't like doesn't matter to me since he was fool enough to let you come all the way to St. Louis without him."

"Really, now?" I said with a raised eyebrow.

"*Really*. And I'd also say that it is my privilege and my duty to take you off his hands."

"Off his hands? You make me sound like I'm some unattended land or something."

"I meant to make you sound like an unguarded treasure."

I rolled my eyes. "Mm-hmm."

"Do you?"

"Do I what?"

"Have a man?"

"No, I don't. Do you have a woman?"

"That depends on whether or not you give me your number."

"That's not an answer."

"No, I don't... *yet*."

I smiled despite myself. "Yet?"

"*Yet*. Now, may I please have your number?"

I sighed. "Okay, but if I give you my number, it doesn't mean we're anything more than friends."

He leaned in until his lips nearly touched mine, looked me dead in the eye, and said, "Then I'll just have to take what I can get until I can change your mind."

I felt his breath against my lips and my pulse quickened. "Uh, w... what makes you think you can make me change my mind?" I asked as his eyes pierced mine.

He backed away from me and smiled. "The fact that you wanted me to kiss you right then."

I put my hands on my hips. "How can you know what I want, sir? You think you can read my mind or something?"

He kept his eyes on mine and gave me a lopsided grin. "Nope, but I can read your body. That gorgeous body of yours cannot lie. You like me—you just don't wanna admit it."

I cleared my throat and rubbed my hand across my afro. I was all out of witty responses because, truthfully, I *did* want him to kiss me. *Did he just say I had a gorgeous body?*

His eyes sparkled as his grin widened. "Number?"

I rattled off my number to him and watched as he programmed it into his cell phone. I unlocked the front door then turned and wished Chris a good night.

"Good night, Marli Meadows. I'ma call you. Oh, and I *love* a challenge."

"I bet you do," I said. I entered the apartment and shut the door behind me.

There was no sign of Carla. *That's odd. I thought I saw her car in the lot outside.* I shrugged and decided that maybe she was still out somewhere with Carolyn and Ronda. After I showered and changed into my night clothes, I headed straight to bed and had no trouble falling asleep.

~*~

I wasn't sure what time Carla made it home, but when I arose the next day, she was already up and in the shower. She told me that she and the other ladies had spent the evening drinking and watching movies at Carolyn's apartment, and when it started getting late, she'd decided to spend the night at her place. I knew she was probably lying but I didn't want to get into another argument with her. So instead, I filled her in on my visit with Chris and his family.

"He's really nice. They all are. But you know, I've just never thought about dating outside my race," I said.

"Well, it's really not as different as you think. A man is a man. Black, white, or orange," Carla replied.

"How would you know there's no difference?"

Carla smiled. "Oh, that's right. I never told you."

I raised my eyebrows. "Told me what?"

"About Steve. I messed around with him that summer I had that internship in Denver."

"Oh, yeah. I remember, that was the summer after your sophomore year in college."

She nodded. "Right."

"So Steve was white?"

"Nope, Asian."

"Asian? You dated an Asian guy?"

"Oh, we did more than date, my dear. A *whole* lot more."

"What?! Ooo, Carla!"

Carla laughed. "I really liked him, you know? But he was all into his education. He wasn't gonna let anything get in the way of that. I missed him for a long time after I got back to Arkansas."

"Hey, weren't you and Bryan together back then, too?"

She raised her eyebrows. "Well, yeah, and I figured what he didn't know wouldn't hurt him. I mean, it's not like we were *married* back then."

I rolled my eyes. "Lord help you, Carla."

"Anyway, I said all that to say this: I think you should give the guy a chance. It ain't like you been strutting around here with Morris Chestnut or somebody."

"Wow, thanks, Carla."

"Look, I'm just being real with you. He's fine as *hell*—he's got this Brad Pitt kind of thing going on except he's got much more swagger. He sounds black, his family's black; hell, he even walks like a black man. It's like you get the best of both worlds. I don't see a problem."

"Carla, I'm being serious."

"Okay, let's get to the important stuff then. He's employed, got a nice ride, and he likes you. I say go for it. Shoot, if it was me, I'd be all over that. Besides, what do you have to lose?"

"Not a thing."

ELEVEN

"EVERY WORD"

True to his word, Chris called me that afternoon shortly before I left for work. We talked for a few minutes and made plans for him to call me later on, during my break. I was happy to hear his voice, and I looked forward to talking to him again. I liked Chris, but then again, he was a hard person to dislike.

Work started out a little slower than usual. I was there for almost an hour before my first patient arrived—a ten-year old who'd been hit in the eye with a baseball during a little league game. I took his history and checked his vital signs, and by the time I made it back to the nurses' station to chart, there had been an influx of patients. The ER was so busy that I missed Chris's call and wasn't able to take my break until much later than usual.

When things finally slowed down, I headed outside, sat on a bench, and dialed Chris's number, hoping that he was still awake.

"Hello?" answered his familiar voice.

I smiled. "Hey, it's Marli. Sorry I missed your call earlier. It's been a zoo here tonight."

"Yeah, I figured. Glad you called me back, though. Where are you? In the cafeteria?"

"No, I'm outside the ER. I needed some air."

"They're working you hard tonight, huh?"

I nodded. "Yeah, they are. I was afraid I'd wake you up. Had you gone to bed yet?"

"No, not yet."

"What are you doing, then?"

"Besides talking to you?"

I laughed. "Yes, besides talking to me."

"Well, right now I'm walking out the doors of the ER lobby, headed your way."

"What?"

I felt a tap on my shoulder and nearly dropped my phone when I saw Chris standing next to me, holding a single yellow rose. He was smiling widely as he lowered his phone from his ear, took a seat next to me on the bench, and handed me the rose.

"Surprised?" he asked.

"Well, yeah. How long have you been here?"

"I've been here a couple of hours hanging out in the canteen. If you hadn't called me back, I was gonna fake chest pains so I could get back there to see you."

I laughed. "Now why would you go to all that trouble just to see me?"

"Because you're special, Ms. Marli, and I missed you."

I shook my head. "Chris, you don't even know me. How can you say you missed me?"

"Okay, since you're all hung up on the fact that I don't know you, how long is your break?"

I checked my watch. "Another fifteen minutes."

"All right, tell me five things about you. When you're finished, I'll tell you five about me."

I sighed. "Okay, um, I'm thirty-three, I have one half-sister. I have an eighteen-year-old daughter, Tiffany. I was married once, and my favorite color is fuchsia."

He nodded. "Well, I'm thirty. I have a son, Russell, who's eight now. Never been married. I was in the marching band in college and, uh, my favorite color is brown."

"I bet it is," I said under my breath.

Chris grinned. "What was that?"

I shook my head. "Oh, nothing. Does your son live here in St.

Louis?"

"Um, I don't know. It's kind of a long, complicated story. Too long for fifteen minutes."

"Actually, it's more like twelve minutes now."

"Okay, where's your daughter?"

"In Atlanta, at Spelman."

"That's good. Great school."

"What school were you in the band at?"

"Grambling."

"You went to Grambling?"

"Yep, on a minority scholarship."

"Get out of here! Are you serious?"

He nodded. "Dead serious. Still go visit for homecoming."

I raised my eyebrows. "Wow, you never cease to amaze me, Mr. King."

He leaned closer to me. "And I'm just getting warmed up, Ms. Meadows. You have no idea the things I can show you."

I smiled and looked away from him. I could feel my cheeks heating up. "Um... were you telling the truth before? You've really never dated a white girl?"

"The truth and nothing but the truth."

"Why?"

He shrugged. "Just my preference. I love black women. Always have."

"I see."

"Mm-hmm. So, what's your favorite thing in the world?" he asked.

"That's easy. Music."

He smiled. "I love music, too. It's good we have that in common. Are you a musician yourself?"

I laughed. "Not unless you count playing the clarinet in junior high school. I wish I was one, though."

"Maybe I could teach you one day."

"Trumpet?"

"Or piano or guitar."

"You play those, too?"

"Yep."

"Okay. Well, maybe so, then."

He smiled and nodded. "I'd be glad to. Who's your favorite singer?"

"Sade. Yours?"

"His purple majesty, himself. Prince!"

I laughed. "Ah, so you're a Prince fan, huh?"

"*Always*. The man knows how to get his point across, you know? You ever listened to 'Adore'? The man is talking some serious stuff. By the end of that song, you feel like he took you to church!"

I grinned. "I'll have to listen to that one again."

"Yeah, you should do that. So, what's your least favorite thing?"

I thought for a moment. "Hmm, people who lie. I *hate* being lied to. That really gets on my nerves."

"Okay, I'll remember that. Not that I'm in the business of lying, anyway."

"Good to know. What about you?"

"My least favorite thing? I guess that would be sleeping alone."

I smiled. "Hmm, I see. Do you sleep with a teddy bear or something?"

He looked me in the eye. "No, I don't."

"So what do you do?"

"I hug my pillow real tight and pretend it's you."

I wrinkled my brow. "Um, is that a come-on, Mr. King?"

He licked his lips and shook his head. "Unh-uh. It's the truth. Ever since we met, I've imagined what it would feel like to hold you and touch you."

He leaned closer, and once again, I could feel his warm breath on my lips. I raised my hand to my chest, trying to hide its rapid rise and fall.

"R... really?"

He nodded. "*Really*. You are the most beautiful woman I've ever seen in my life," he whispered.

I dropped my eyes, suddenly feeling shy. "Um, th... thank you."

He moved his head and kissed me on the cheek. I released the breath I'd been holding.

He stood and reached for my hand. "Come on, let me walk you back inside before I get you in trouble." That statement definitely had a double meaning.

He walked me to the employee entrance and kissed my hand, then he pointed to the rose he'd given me. "That's a friendship rose, or at least that's what the florist said. The next time I give you a rose it won't be yellow."

"How do you know there'll be a next time?"

"Oh, there will be. I can guarantee it."

I shook my head and smiled. He had enough confidence for the both of us. "Okay, so what color will the next rose be?"

He smiled. "You'll see when I give it to you. Good night, Marli."

I watched as he turned and walked away. "Good night, Chris," I whispered.

~*~

Tuesday brought a day of much needed sleep and another hectic night of work. This time, I managed to take my break at the regular time and spent every minute of it talking on the phone to Chris, as I did my lunch and my second break. Somehow, we never ran out of things to talk about—and the more I learned about him, the more I liked him. He told me he had a degree in music education and had been with The St. Louis Kingsmen as a founding member and manager for five years. The band, which consisted mostly of some high school buddies of his, travelled all over the country, but their largest following was at home in St. Louis. Before the formation of The St. Louis Kingsmen, he taught music at a high school.

He was both intelligent and smooth. He loved to talk but was also a very attentive listener. When he told me the band would be leaving for Memphis on that Wednesday, I can honestly say that I hated for him to go. I knew I'd miss him, but he assured me he'd be back by that Friday night. We made plans to see each other on Saturday.

Wednesday and Thursday were my off nights for the week, and I looked forward to watching a movie with Carla or just hanging around the apartment with her and catching up.

Evidently, Carla had different plans. By the time I crawled out of bed late Wednesday morning, she was already gone. The only trace of her was a note informing me that she'd be back in time for work Friday night. I knew she couldn't be with Quinton since he was on the road with Chris. God only knew where she was or who she was with. I decided I wouldn't confront her about her behavior anymore, realizing that it would only alienate her and put her on the defensive. I just prayed for her safety and hoped she'd eventually come to herself.

I guess it's just me, I thought. I ended up spending the evening listening to music. I listened to "Adore" by Prince about six times before finally drifting off to sleep on the couch. Around 1:00 A.M., I was awakened by the ringing of my cell phone.

I sat up on the couch and answered with a nervous, groggy, "Hello?" I hadn't had the presence of mind to check the caller ID. I hoped nothing had happened to Tiffany or Carla.

"Hey, did I wake you?" It was Chris on the other end.

I squinted and checked the time on the screen of my phone. "Well, yeah. Chris? Is everything okay?"

"Are you worried about me, Ms. Meadows? That's sweet."

"Chris, it's 1:00 A.M. What's going on?"

"Sorry about that. We just finished our last set and one of the songs made me think of you. So I had to call you."

"What? Y'all played a song called 'Marli'?"

He chuckled. "No. Can I play it for you?"

"Over the phone? Where are you?"

"In my room, at the hotel."

"You're gonna play your trumpet at the hotel at this time of morning? Do they allow that? They might kick you out or something," I said through a yawn.

He laughed again. "I'ma just play a little bit. Maybe it won't be bad enough for them to throw me out."

I rubbed my eyes. "Okay. Well, go ahead."

"All right."

I leaned back against the sofa and closed my eyes as he began to play. I quickly recognized the song. It was one of my favorites and before I knew it, I was humming along with the melody. Chris's trumpet sounded beautiful. He played so well that I really wished he wouldn't stop. I smiled when he picked up the phone and sang a line from the song.

"That was beautiful," I said. "That's one of my favorite Michael Jackson songs."

"Ah, so you know it?" he asked, sounding a little surprised. "Not many people know that one."

"Well, 'I Can't Help It' is actually my favorite song from the *Off the Wall* album. But then again, I like most all of MJ's stuff."

"Yeah, me, too. Esperanza Spalding did a good job with that song, too."

"Did she? I'll have to check her version out. So, um… what are you trying to tell me? What can't you help?"

"I can't help thinking about you. Woman, you linger on my mind," he said huskily.

I felt another smile begin to creep upon my lips. "Really, now?"

"*Really*. There's something about you that makes me think I don't wanna let you slip away from me."

Dang, this guy was smooth. "You know, Chris? You sure can talk a good game."

"Naw, no game. I'm 100% serious. I mean what I say. Something inside of me is not gonna let me rest until you're mine."

"What if I told you that won't happen?"

"I'd say that I don't believe you."

"I'm only here for another six weeks, Chris. And then what?"

"And then I convince you to stay."

"You're awfully sure of yourself."

"The only thing I'm sure of is this connection I feel between us. You feel it, too. You just don't wanna admit it."

"Presumptions and assumptions. You jump to a lot of conclusions, don't you?"

"No, I don't, Marli. If you didn't like me, you wouldn't be on the phone with me at one in the morning, now would you?"

"Whatever, Chris," I replied with a grin on my face so huge, he could probably see it through the phone.

"Uh-huh, I got you dead to rights. Anyway, I'ma let you go. I gotta read my Bible, pray, and then get some rest. Good night, 'Mean Marli.'"

I laughed. "Good night, 'Cool Chris.'"

"And you know this," he said before hanging up the phone.

I sat there for a moment with a silly smile on my face, feeling like a teenager. Speaking of teenagers, I stared at my phone and wondered about Tiffany. I'd left a couple of messages and had only received a text from her telling me she was fine, but busy, and would call when she had a chance. I sighed and said a prayer for her before heading to bed for the rest of the night, or, morning, actually.

TWELVE

"KISS OF LIFE"

Thursday zipped by and I was kind of glad that it did. Carla had been MIA except for a few chain text messages, and I was beginning to feel a little lonely. Chris's phone calls had been my only consolation. I was definitely looking forward to seeing him again. He was really beginning to grow on me and I knew that when I returned home to Arkansas, I'd miss him.

I spent most of Friday reading a novel, trying to rest up for a weekend of work, and thinking about my life back in Arkansas. To be honest, I really didn't miss it at all. I had called my mother a couple of times, but other than that, I hadn't had any contact with anyone back home. If I was real with myself, I'd have to admit that with Tiffany all grown up and gone off to college, there was really nothing tying me to Arkansas.

Maybe I could stay here a little longer.

I shook my head at my own thoughts. Was I actually considering staying in St. Louis to be around some guy I'd only known a couple of weeks? That would be worse than what Carla was doing.

As if I'd conjured her up in my thoughts, Carla arrived back at the apartment about three hours before our shift at the hospital.

"Hey," I said, being as friendly as I could. But she was really getting on my last nerve.

"Hey, girl," she said cheerfully.

I picked up the book I'd been reading and tried to ignore her. I was doing my best to avoid a confrontation with her.

"So, what you been up to?" she asked.

"Not a thing," I said tersely.

She sighed. "Okay, so you're mad at me again. Look, I'm here way before our shift. I didn't leave you hanging this time."

"Gee, thanks for the consideration, Carla. I really appreciate it."

She plopped down on the couch. "Look, Marli, I'm not gonna just sit around here and twiddle my thumbs. I've done enough of that. It's time for me to live. I'm doing *me* now."

I lowered my book and looked her in the eye. "Humph, seems to me like you're doing everyone else, too."

She let out an exasperated sigh. "Look, Greg offered to take me to Chicago with him for a couple of days and I took him up on his offer."

I frowned. "Who the hell is Greg?"

"Oh, yeah. You don't know him. I met him at the church last Sunday."

My frown deepened. "You went to Chicago and spent two nights with a guy you met at *church*? What are you doing, Carla?"

She shrugged. "He paid for everything, and I had a great time. I'm a grown woman, and I'm not doing anything wrong."

"I bet you paid for it one way or another."

Carla squeezed her eyes shut and shook her head. "Ugh! There you go judging again! I'm not doing anything any other single woman wouldn't do."

I rose up on the couch. "That's just it! *You are not single, Carla!* You're wildin' the freak out! I don't understand you. You've cornered the market on selfishness and inconsideration. I mean, you've just thrown all caution to the wind. Is this the way you're gonna act when we get back home or is this just your 'St. Louis persona'?"

She was as cool as a cucumber as she said, "Who said I was going back home?"

"Carla, you've got your boys to raise. What are you talking about? You've *gotta* go back!"

She waved her hand in the air as if dismissing my comment. "Hell, Bryan can raise 'em. I was doing everything for them before *and* after we separated. It's his turn now."

Was she serious? I searched her eyes. Her expression was so cold, I had to look away. "Carla, those are your sons, your *babies*. You act like we're discussing the family pet or something. You can't mean what you're saying."

She nodded. "Oh yeah, I mean it. Tell me, what did sacrificing your life and happiness to raise Tiffany get you? She's called you, what, two times since you've been here? I'm not doing that to myself. I'm gonna enjoy my life while I still can."

I was speechless. She was really going for the jugular to prove her point. She was using my life as some type of an example of what *not* to do.

I sat there and stared at her for a moment and then I stood and left for my bedroom. I shut the door behind me, collapsed onto the bed, and cried. She was right about one thing—I *had* sacrificed my life for Tiffany's happiness. I'd also bitten my tongue far too many times trying to stay on everyone's good side, and the product of it all was my own misery.

I didn't agree with what Carla was doing, but I could see how she could've reached that point of selfishness and I could see how her actions mirrored my own. To be honest, what Carla was doing was tame compared to what I did after my divorce. Maybe that's why her behavior was bothering me so much. Maybe watching what she was doing reminded me too much of myself. Lord knows, I wanted to help her, but truthfully, I needed just as much help as she did.

~*~

Friday night was so ridiculously hectic that I didn't have the energy to have lunch with Chris on Saturday as we'd planned. Saturday night wasn't much better, and I don't even want to discuss Sunday night. I was relieved when my shift was over Monday morning, and I was thrilled to make it home and crawl into bed.

Carla and I really hadn't spoken to each other much since our last conversation. We'd both been so exhausted from work that we'd mostly just moved around the apartment in silence. Our rides to and from work were tense and silent as well. I really, *really* regretted not driving my own car to St. Louis.

Monday morning, I'd planned to sleep most of the day and get up and call Chris that evening. Well, my plans were thwarted pretty quickly. Maybe thwarted is not a good word to use, but they were certainly altered. Around noon, I heard banging on the front door. I rolled over in bed without opening my eyes, hoping that Carla would answer it since it was probably for her anyway.

The banging continued, and finally, I sat up in bed. Disgusted, I grabbed my robe and wrapped it around me as I schlepped to the front door, ready to cuss out whoever had disturbed my much-needed sleep.

I swung the door open without even checking the peep hole and said, "Yes?!" in as disgusted a tone as I could muster.

There, standing on the other side of the door, was Chris looking *too* good, grinning from ear to ear, his hands in the pockets of his jeans. His clothes fit him so well, I was beginning to wonder if he had them specially made or something.

"Did I wake you?" he asked.

"Well, yeah, me and probably Carla, too."

"Nah, not Carla. I just saw her downstairs, getting in the car with Quinton."

I shook my head. "Figures."

"Can I come in?"

I stood there for a moment, staring at the fit of those jeans he was wearing. Then I came to myself. "Uh, yeah, come on in."

I backed out of the doorway and allowed him to enter the apartment. As he passed me, his cologne filled my nostrils. He looked *and* smelled good, and at that point, I was really feeling me some Chris King.

I offered him a seat on the sofa and sat down next to him before realizing I was only wearing my nightshirt and robe. I rubbed my hand across the scarf that covered my head. I must've looked a hot mess.

"Hey, let me take a quick shower and get decent," I said.

He nodded. "Okay, dress comfortably. I've got a lot to show you today."

I raised my eyebrows. "What makes you think I'm going anywhere with you?"

"Because you are," he said, then brought his face close to mine and looked me in the eye.

I watched as his eyes slowly fell to my lips. We sat there for a moment—me holding my breath with my eyes glued to him, him with his eyes glued to my lips. And then he kissed me—slowly, softly. As he pulled away from me, he gently tugged on my bottom lip with his teeth. And with his eyes still on my mouth he said, "I knew it."

"You... you knew what?" I asked as I tried to catch my breath.

"I knew your lips were soft."

"Oh, uh, thank you."

He lifted his gaze to my eyes and smiled. "You're welcome."

We sat there and stared at each other. I wanted to look away, but I couldn't. "Um, I think I was about to do something," I whispered.

He nodded. "You were gonna get dressed so we can head out."

"Oh, yeah, I... I'll be right back," I stammered as I left the living room. I stumbled and had to grab the wall as I walked down the hall to my room.

For some reason, I was trembling as I showered. It must've been that kiss, because I swear I felt electricity when his lips met mine. I felt tingly in places I'd forgotten even existed on my body. It was as if he'd jump-started every part of me.

As I toweled off, I searched through my closet and finally settled on a pair of jeans that fit my wide hips just right, a sleeveless red blouse that showed just the right amount of my ample cleavage, and a comfortable pair of gold sandals. I quickly dressed, picked out my 'fro, put on some gold hoop earrings, and headed back to the living room. If that kiss was any indication of how things with Chris were going to be, I couldn't wait for more!

Chris stood to his feet and shook his head when I entered the room. "My, my, my, Ms. Meadows. Don't you look *beautiful*."

I looked down at my outfit and shrugged. "It's just some jeans and a blouse, but thank you."

He walked over to me, took my hand, and kissed it. "You sure do wear it well."

I dropped my eyes and tried to hide the giddiness that was rising up inside of me. "Um, thanks, again."

He smiled down at me. "Come on, let's go."

I followed Chris out of the apartment and we walked to his car hand-in-hand. Once we were in his car, I asked, "Where are we going?"

"Well, I figured we'd grab something to eat and head to Pacific."

"Pacific? Is that a town?"

Chris glanced at me and smiled. "Yeah, it's a little under an hour away. There's something there that I wanna show you."

I nodded. *I bet there's a lot you could show me.*

"But if you wanna see the Pacific Ocean, that can be arranged, too."

"Hmm, so are you saying that my wish is your command?" I asked as I gave him a little side-eye.

He shot me a sly grin. "All day, every day, baby."

I tried not to smile as I turned my head and gazed out the window. I tried and failed.

After grabbing a couple of biscuits at a fast food restaurant, we hit the highway, headed toward a destination unknown to me. The conversation was light along the way until I asked a question that had been burning my brain.

"Chris, what did you mean when you said you didn't know if your son lived here?" I asked.

His grip on the steering wheel tightened and the smile he always wore disappeared from his face. "Um, it's a long story."

I reached over and placed my hand gently on his arm. "We've got time. Tell me."

Chris took a deep breath and slowly released it. "Um, well, I met his mom, Fatima, back in college. She was from St. Louis, too. We were together a couple of years, and after I graduated, she moved to Texas with me. I'd gotten a job teaching music at a high school there. I really cared about her and was thinking about marrying her. So anyway, she got pregnant after we'd been there about a year. When Russ was born, my life changed in so many ways.

"I asked Fatima to marry me, but she said she wasn't ready. It seemed like while I was trying to settle down and grow up, she did the exact opposite. After she had Russ, she started staying out late, disappearing for days at a time. Later on, her mother told me that mental illness ran in her family. She said that Fatima had been dealing with some emotional issues for years. I never saw it in her until she had Russ, though. Anyway, when Russ was about eighteen months old, she up and left. Moved in with some guy she'd met and left Russ with me."

He paused and shook his head. "My parents eventually talked me into coming back home so they could help me with the baby. I got a place here and quit working so I could spend more time with him.

He had a lot of respiratory infections and ended up being diagnosed with asthma, so I liked to stay close to him.

"When Russ was three, Fatima called me crying, saying that her boyfriend had left her and that she had nowhere to go. She said she missed me and Russell. So like a dummy, I sent her a ticket and flew her back here."

"You weren't dumb. She was your son's mother and you just wanted to help her," I said.

"Yeah, well, true to form, she bit the hand that fed her. She was only here for like five months before she ran off again. Only this time, she took Russell with her and moved in with some drug dealer. I tried to get him back, but since we were never married and had no legal custody agreement, there was nothing I could really do. I decided to sue for custody and won—mostly because she didn't even bother to show up for court. When the police went with me to pick Russell up, she'd left. She's been on the run ever since. There's even an Amber Alert out for him. I've hired all kinds of private detectives, but I haven't found him yet. It's... it's like they just disappeared.

"I catch myself looking for him all the time—on the internet or when I'm out and about. I'll see a little boy and wonder. And I worry about him, wonder if his mother is taking care of him, who's around him, how they're treating him. It's hard, Marli. It's the worst thing I've ever been through."

I rubbed his arm. "I'm so sorry, Chris. How long has it been since you've seen him?"

"Five years. He probably doesn't even remember me. I miss him *so much*."

"I can't imagine how you must feel. I'm so very sorry."

He sighed. "Yeah, well, all I can do is pray and believe that God is watching over him and that one day I'll get him back."

I nodded. "I believe you will."

He looked over at me, pain in his eyes. "Thanks, Marli."

After a few more minutes of driving, Chris finally pulled into a parking lot.

"Where are we?" I asked as I climbed out of his car.

"At the famous St. Louis Grottos. The home of the Black Madonna."

"Okay…"

He chuckled. "Come on, you'll see."

I shrugged and took his hand as he led the way. We walked through the open-air chapel, and before I knew it, we were approaching an absolutely stunning structure. If you looked closely, you could see that it was made of rock, sea shells, and costume jewelry.

"What do they call this one?" I asked.

"That's the Our Lady of Perpetual Help Grotto," said Chris. We passed one beautiful sculptural display of artwork after another, and as I listened to Chris discuss their history, I couldn't help but to be awestruck.

"One man really made all of this?" I asked.

"With God's help," Chris answered. "That's why I like coming here. It shows me that we can do anything we put our minds to with God's help."

I nodded and continued to take in the beauty of one display after the other—St. Joseph's Grotto, the Gethsemane Grotto, and the Nativity Grotto were all absolutely beautiful. As we approached the portrait of the Black Madonna, I smiled.

"She's brown," I whispered. I turned and smiled at Chris.

His eyes were glued to me as he said, "And she's beautiful."

We finished our tour and headed to the gift shop where I bought a couple of souvenirs. Afterward, we walked back to Chris's car.

"Thank you for bringing me here, Chris," I said as I fastened my seat belt.

He reached over and gently caressed my cheek. "You're welcome, Ms. Marli."

He stared at me for a moment. I stared right back, and as he held my undivided attention, he leaned in and slowly covered my mouth with his. He cupped my face in his hands as he deepened the kiss. I pushed my hand against the dashboard to brace myself. He kissed me like he'd not only taken a course in kissing at Grambling, but had majored in it and graduated summa cum laude.

As he caressed my mouth with his, the only words in mind were *Good. Lord.* When he finally released me, I leaned back in my seat and caught my breath.

I rubbed my finger across my lips. Every single inch of my body was standing at attention. "Um-uh, what was that for?"

He shrugged. "Your lips looked like they needed it."

I smiled and shook my head. "You are definitely like no one I've ever known before."

"What? Because I'm white?"

"No, because you're *you*. You're Chris King, and there's nobody else like you—black or white."

He raised his eyebrows. "And what's your opinion of Chris King?"

"I like him."

He started the engine with a smile. "Told you so."

THIRTEEN

"LOVERS ROCK"

Chris spent the remainder of the day showing me around St. Louis. He showed me everything he could think of from his old schools to his old hang-out spots. That evening, we had dinner with his parents, and I was thoroughly entertained by their stories of Chris as a smart, talented, but somewhat mischievous child.

Tuesday, bright and early, Chris picked me up and took me to the Gateway Arch Riverfront, where we explored the museum and took a riverboat ride. By that evening, I was exhausted but had thoroughly enjoyed my day with Chris.

"Okay, time for dinner," he said as I collapsed into his car.

"Oh, where's dinner tonight?" I asked.

He gave me a wide grin. "It's a surprise."

"You're just always full of surprises aren't you, Mr. King?"

"Gotta be if I'ma keep up with you, Mean Marli."

I grinned and shook my head.

A few minutes later, we pulled into a gas station. "Gotta gas up. Sit tight," Chris said and then leaned over and kissed me softly. I smiled and watched as he walked into the gas station.

I'd pulled out my cell phone and was checking for missed calls when I heard a tap on my window. There was a young, black guy whom I didn't recognize standing next to the car, peering inside at me. *Maybe he's a friend of Chris's.* I turned the key in the ignition, rolled the window down, and said, "Yes?"

The guy shook his head. "Really, sister?"

I frowned. "Do I know you?"

"Naw, but I know *you*. You one of them sisters who thinks rolling around with some white dude is the thing to do. Brothers ain't good enough for you, huh? But if I had a white girl on my arm, you'd have a fit, wouldn't you?"

"What? Who the hell *are* you?"

He nodded slowly. "Yeah, I know your type. He riding you around in a Benz, prolly paying your bills. I bet it's all about the money, ain't it? That's all y'all want—somebody to foot the bills for you."

I shook my head and rolled the window back up. I didn't have time for that mess, and who I was with was none of this stranger's business.

He threw his hands up and I could hear him through the window as he continued, "Dang, it's like that? I hope you come to your senses and come back to the *black* side, my sister."

I glared at him and mouthed, *"Go away."*

The guy shook his head and then pounded his fist on the roof of the car before walking away. I jumped and checked to be sure my door was locked. I was still a little shaken up when Chris made it back to the car.

He opened the door, threw his wallet on the seat, and said, "Who was that dude you were talking to?"

I shrugged. "I… I don't know. Just some guy."

Chris looked at me for a moment. "What'd he say?"

I shifted my eyes from Chris's face. "Nothing."

"He must've said something. He was standing here for a good minute."

"It… it was nothing. Just pump the gas so we can go."

Chris stood there and eyed me for a moment and then he turned and looked at the guy, who was busy pumping gas—his back to us as he leaned against his car.

"Son of a—oh, *hell* naw!" Chris fumed. He slammed his door shut and began walking toward the guy's car. "Ay!"

I fumbled with the door handle. *Oh, Lord.*

I finally got my door open, scrambled to my feet outside the car, and yelled, "Chris!"

Chris, who'd already reached the guy's car, said, "I'll be right back, Marli."

He didn't turn around, but walked around the vehicle until he stood face-to-face with the guy. Chris was taller than him and bigger than him, and at that point I had no doubt that he could've whooped the guy's butt, but I knew I'd have a hard time explaining to Chris's parents why he was in jail for assault.

"Ay, man! The hell you say to my woman?" Chris asked.

The guy looked over at me and then at Chris. The look in his eye told me that he, too, figured that Chris could whoop his butt. "Man, go on with that," the guy said.

Chris folded his arms across his chest. "Naw, man. You got something to say, you need to say it to me, *not* her."

"Chris!" I yelled. *"Let's go!"*

Chris shook his head but never took his eyes off of the guy. "Get back in the car, Marli."

The guy raised his hands. "Look, man, listen to your woman. I ain't got no beef with you. *She's* the traitor."

Chris dropped his arms and raised his voice. "What the hell does that mean? *Traitor?*"

"Chris! Chris *come on!*" I shouted and then began walking toward them.

"Baby, get in the car. I'll be right there," Chris said.

"*Baby?* I got you wrong, huh, playa? She done blackified you. Look, my bad, man. Didn't mean no disrespect. Like I said, my beef ain't with you, it's with her."

"You got beef with her, you got beef with me," Chris said evenly.

I finally reached them and grabbed Chris's arm. "*Chris, please, let's just go. He is not worth all of this trouble.*"

Chris looked at me and then back at the guy. He shook his head. "You're right." He glanced at the guy as we walked away. Then he stopped and turned around. "Don't make the mistake of disrespecting my girl, again, man."

We made it to the car and I climbed inside and sighed with relief. Chris pumped the gas, staring the guy down until he drove away. When he finally climbed back into the car, I tore into him. "Are you crazy?! That guy could've had a gun or some buddies lurking around the corner, waiting to jump on you. You must've been out of your mind, getting up in his face like that!"

He shook his head. "Naw, I knew he wasn't dangerous. He was a coward, that's why he confronted you and not me. I could've easily whooped him up."

I turned and looked out the window. "That ego of yours is gonna get you hurt one day, and I don't wanna be the one to witness it when it happens."

"It's not like I started it. He shouldn't have disrespected you."

I released a frustrated sigh. "*Chris...*"

He sighed and after a moment of silence said, "I'm sorry, Marli."

I closed my eyes and rested my head against the back of the seat. "Fine. Let's just go."

I felt his hand as he caressed my cheek. "Marli, look at me."

I opened my eyes and turned my head toward him. He kissed me softly on the lips. "I'm really sorry, okay?"

"I said it was fine, Chris. Can we just go?"

Chris reached over and grasped my hand. "You mad at me?"

I sighed. "No, I'm not mad."

"Good."

He smiled as he started the car and pulled back onto the street.

About twenty minutes later, Chris drove into a parking deck downtown, parked his car, and led me to the building next door. We entered what looked like a hotel lobby and I started to feel a little apprehensive. Why was he taking me to a hotel? What did he really have planned?

I was beginning to feel more than a little disappointed. I believed that Chris was different, that he was after more than just sex. My face dropped along with my spirits as we boarded the elevator. And as disappointed as I was in Chris, I was even more disappointed in myself for not insisting that he take me home. But it was like I couldn't make myself say it, and I couldn't control my own feet. It was as if the old me, the expert booty-caller me, had taken over.

"This is where I live. I have a condo upstairs, fifth floor," he said as he pressed a button on the panel. I watched as the five lit up.

"Oh, okay." I still didn't quite know what to think.

"You scurred?" he asked, leaning in close to my ear.

"No," I said defensively.

"Yeah, you were. You thought we were in some hotel and I was gonna try to have my way with you, didn't you?"

"No, I didn't," I said, sounding pretty unconvincing.

He leaned over and planted a long kiss on my lips, then whispered in my ear, "God knows I want to, but I respect you, Marli. I think we're working toward something more than just sex."

Can this man get any better? I reached up and returned his kiss with one of my own. After a few seconds, our lips parted, and as I stepped back, Chris grabbed me and held me close as he kissed me deeply. I thought I'd melt right then and there. With his kiss, he'd rocked me right to my core, and the only thought in my head was that I didn't want him to stop.

When the elevator doors opened, he finally released me and we squeezed past a young white couple who was standing outside the doors. I could see them giving us odd looks, but Chris didn't seem to notice as he grabbed my hand and guided me down the hall.

He unlocked the door to apartment 5E. "Welcome to my humble abode, Ms. Meadows."

I smiled and followed him inside. As I looked around the place, my eyes widened. "Humble" was definitely not how I'd describe it. "Gorgeous" would be more appropriate. I followed Chris through the foyer into the living room and felt as if I'd walked into an interior designer's lab. The walls were painted a deep, creamy shade of beige. Modern, expensive-looking furniture decorated the room in shades of bronze, rust, and camel. On the walls hung poster-sized black and white photos of the city.

"Have a seat," he said, gesturing toward a comfortable-looking leather sofa.

"Okay. Chris, your place is *beautiful*. Did you decorate it yourself?"

Chris shook his head. "Nah, paid a decorator to do it."

"Well, it was money well spent. This place is gorgeous."

"Thanks. So feel free to look around. I'ma go and get started on dinner."

"Wait, are you cooking for us?" I asked.

"I sure am," he replied and then turned and glided off to the kitchen.

I sat there for a moment, took in my surroundings, and noticed some photos lining a bookshelf across the room. I walked over to get a closer look and smiled at the row of pictures that gave me a glimpse into Chris's past. Some were copies of the ones at his parents' home, others I'd never seen before—one of which was a really nice photo of Chris in his graduation cap and gown, surrounded by his sisters. I picked it up to get a closer look.

"Graduation day at Grambling," he said. I hadn't noticed him standing behind me.

He pointed to the faces. "That's Jayne. I know you haven't met her yet, and of course you know Ava and Lana."

I nodded. "Ava, Lana, and Jayne. Beautiful names for beautiful women."

"Yeah, my mom's an old movie fanatic, in case you haven't figured that out. She once told me that if I hadn't already been named Christopher, she would've named me Humphrey."

I raised my eyebrows. "Like Humphrey Bogart? Well, thank God she didn't get a chance to."

He nodded. "Amen."

I continued to peruse the pictures and came to one in particular that caught my eye. It was of a little boy who was obviously of mixed race. He had fair, brown skin and curly, black hair. His striking blue eyes told me that he was Chris's son, Russell.

I picked the picture up for a closer look. "Is this—"

"Yeah, that's Russ," he said, softly.

"He's a beautiful child. He has your eyes."

He nodded, his eyes full of sadness. "Yeah, he does. Thank you."

"I didn't notice any photos of him at your parents' house."

He shook his head. "No, Mama took them down. It was just too painful for her to see him all the time. She worries about him a lot. He was her first grandchild."

"You'll get him back, Chris. I'm sure of it."

"Thanks, Marli."

I moved on to a photo of a white couple. The man looked to be older than the woman. He was tall with dark hair and eyes. The woman was stunningly beautiful with long blond hair and blue eyes.

"These are your real parents?" I asked.

He nodded. "Yeah, Ted and Pamela Russell."

"You look just like your mother."

"Yeah, same eyes, huh?" He stared at the picture for a moment and then said, "So dinner should be ready in about forty-five minutes. Wanna have a seat with me?"

"You're cooking from in here?"

"It's on a timer." He hesitated and then added, "I'm really sorry about losing my cool earlier."

"It's okay. I just didn't want you to get in any trouble. That guy definitely was not worth it."

"I know."

I smiled slyly. "For a preacher's kid, you got a little street in you, huh?"

He shrugged and dropped his eyes.

"You called me your woman, too."

He looked up at me and raised his eyebrows. "You liked that, huh?"

"Cool Chris" was back.

I nodded and took a seat on the sofa. No sooner than he sat down beside me, Chris pulled me into his arms and laid one heck of a kiss on me. I leaned into him and returned the kiss, rubbing my hands through his hair. It felt different, I can't lie. The texture of his skin, his hair, his lips; it was all different, but it was good, *very* good.

We kissed and held each other for a long time. It felt good to be able to share that kind of intimacy again. I could feel his affection and passion for me, but it felt innocent, almost pure. It reminded me of the joy and excitement I felt in my younger days, when I liked a boy and knew that he liked me. Back then, there was this sense of excitement I felt just from being around that person or holding his hand. Just a simple kiss was totally thrilling to me. That's what I felt with Chris—the innocence and excitement of a first love.

Chris pulled me closer to him as he continued the kiss, his hands navigating a trail from my back to my waist to my face, as if he wasn't sure which part of me he wanted to touch. I felt the same way—overwhelmed by the chemistry and electricity flowing between us. I didn't want to stop, and I could tell that the feeling was mutual. Had the oven timer not gone off, there's no telling where the night would have led us, despite Chris's honorable intentions.

~*~

Dinner was actually pretty good. Now, he couldn't cook like his mama, but his T-bone steaks, baked potatoes, and spring mix salad weren't half bad. We laughed and talked throughout dinner and afterward, we settled down on his sofa with a couple of sodas and listened to some old-school R&B records. I leaned back on the sofa and sipped my drink as Chris walked over to the stereo to change the record.

"You know, I've always heard that musicians are usually broke, but you've done really well," I said, looking around at the room.

"Uh, yeah. I just manage my money really well," he said, his back to me.

"Well, you need to teach me a thing or two about money management, then."

He turned and smiled at me. "Or three or four, huh?"

"Unh-uh, let's not forget, I'm older and wiser than you. Now when it comes to certain things, I think I have a hand up on you."

He grinned. "That's right, you *are* older than me. That's just how I like my women, old and thick and mean."

I laughed. "Now look, I haven't been mean to you in days. Cut me some slack here."

"Well, when you *were* mean to me, you were mean as *hell*. I ain't never had to work so hard to get a woman before."

I raised my eyebrows. "Oh, so you think you've got me?"

He walked over to me, reached for my hand, and pulled me to my feet. "I *know* I got you. Come on and dance with me."

"Your Love Is King" by Sade began to play. "Well, since this is my favorite song, I guess I will."

"Favorite song, huh? I'll have to remember that," he said as he pulled me into his arms.

I leaned against his chest as he wrapped his long arms around me.

"You're a perfect fit," he whispered.

As we slowly rocked to the music, I could feel my entire body begin to relax against his. I closed my eyes and breathed in the scent of his cologne. He released me long enough to lean over and plant a soft kiss on my lips. I looked up at him and smiled.

"How tall are you?" I asked.

"Six-one. How *short* are you?"

I laughed. "Five-four."

"Perfect," he said and then pulled me back to him. He began to softly sing along with the song.

"Why don't you ever sing lead with the band?"

He looked down at me. "Man, you're full of questions tonight, huh?"

I shrugged. "Just curious."

"I really don't know. I guess I'd just rather play my horn. I don't really like all of the attention on me."

I smiled. "I find that hard to believe, Cool Chris."

"I'm serious. I've always kinda stood out. These days, I like fading into the background with my horn."

I nodded. "You know, Chris, I really envy you."

"Envy me? Why?"

I rested my head on his chest again. "Because you live your life exactly the way you want to. You had dreams of being a musician, and you made them come true. I just gave up on my dreams."

He looked down at me and frowned. "I live this way because it's the only way I know how to live. If you let go of your dreams, you stop really living. Living without fighting for your dreams is not living at all—that's just existing."

I sighed. "That's what I've been doing for so many years. *Existing*."

Chris stopped dancing and cupped my face with his hands. "What do you dream about, baby? What do you want to do with your life?"

"If I tell you, you'll think it's stupid."

"No, I won't. No dream is ever stupid."

"Well, the only thing I've ever dreamed of doing is falling in love—*real love*—and having a family. I wanted to be a stay at home mom and bake cookies and fix huge meals for my family. I know it sounds archaic, but I guess I wanted that because I never had it growing up. My parents always emphasized education and having a big career, but I never cared about that. The things I've always wanted and never had are love and family."

"That's not stupid, baby. That's beautiful."

"It *would* be beautiful if it was a dream that could actually come true."

"What makes you think it can't?"

I shrugged again. "I don't know. I guess I feel like it's too late. I'm not getting any younger."

"So you think there's an age limit on love and happiness?"

"Not necessarily. I just think it's too late for *me*. I've got a grown daughter now, too late to be trying to start another family. It's too late for my happily ever after. I just don't believe it'll happen for me."

"Naw, baby. It's only too late if you decide it is. I think as long as you are living and breathing, anything is possible. *Anything,* if you open your heart and mind to it—including a happily ever after. You have no idea what God's got in store for you." And with that, he leaned in and let his lips barely brush mine.

We danced and danced until we were both too tired to move, and then we collapsed onto the couch.

I woke up the next morning on the couch with Chris's arms around me. I looked up at him and smiled. "Good morning," I said softly.

He peered down at me and kissed the tip of my nose. "Good morning, beautiful. You wanna watch the sunrise with me?"

"Sure."

I followed him out onto the balcony, and there we stood, hand in hand, watching a gorgeous, orange sun rise over St. Louis.

"The heavens declare the glory of God; the skies proclaim the work of his hands," he whispered, reciting Psalm 19:1—one of my favorite scriptures.

I squeezed his hand as we took in the breathtaking view. It was the first time in my entire life I'd ever seen a sunrise and it was absolutely beautiful.

FOURTEEN

"THE SWEETEST TABOO"

It was another hectic night at work, and when break time finally came, I decided to hide out in a far corner of the ER lobby. I sat down and dialed Chris's number.

"Hello?" he answered softly.

"Hey, did I wake you?"

"Nah, just stretching. How's your night been?"

"Don't even ask."

"That bad, huh? I bet you were ready for your break."

"I was, and I was ready to hear your voice, too."

"Really? You wanna see my face?"

I smiled. "Yeah, I'd love to."

"And kiss my lips?"

My smile widened. "Mm-hmm."

"Your wish is my command. Come outside."

My smile grew even wider, if that's possible. "Why?"

"Just come outside, woman."

I walked outside but didn't see Chris's car anywhere. "Where are you?" I asked.

"Turn around."

I spun around to find Chris leaning against the outside wall of the ER. Somehow, I'd passed right by him without noticing him. With a grin on his face, he walked over to me and kissed my cheek.

"What are you doing here?" I asked, although I was thrilled to see him.

"I missed you."

"Aw, I missed you, too. You wanna join me in the lobby?"

"Nah, I was thinking that maybe we could have a little make-out session in my car. I'm parked right over there." He pointed to the middle of the parking lot where I could see his shiny Mercedes.

"Make-out session? Wow, you really *are* white. You almost had me fooled there for a minute."

"Aw, now, there you go with that again. Come on."

He took my hand and led me across the parking lot to his car. Once safely inside the back seat, he locked the doors, tuned his cell phone to some soothing sounds on Pandora radio, and before I could get settled in the seat good, his lips were covering mine. As he pulled me into his arms, my heart began to race. His touch excited me. *Everything* about him excited me. My heart was beating so hard I could feel in my throat. I wondered if he could feel it, too.

I was so lost in his embrace that I forgot where I was for a moment. I grabbed the back of his head and leaned into the kiss as Chris tightened his grip on my waist. When he finally released me, I had to gasp for air.

"Okay, so you really *did* miss me, huh?" he said breathily.

"Just a little bit."

"Dang, girl. I need to go away for a few days and see what I get if you miss me a lot."

"I could say the same thing."

He sat there and stared at me for a moment as the music continued to play. "You are so beautiful, Marli."

I dropped my eyes. "Thank you."

"Why do you always do that?"

"Do what?"

"Whenever I tell you you're beautiful, you look away."

"I do?" I shrugged. "I don't know. I guess it's because no one's ever told me I was beautiful before."

He reached over and slid his fingertip gently across my eyebrow, then my eyelid, then my nose, cheek, and lips. "Then everyone around you must've been blind." He leaned in and brushed his lips across mine. "Because you are absolutely beautiful."

I looked into his eyes. "Thank you."

"You are most welcome. I got something for you."

I smiled. "Really? What?"

"This." He reached into the front seat and retrieved a single red rose.

"It's lovely. Thank you."

He smiled. "You're welcome. Remember when I told you your next rose would be a different color?"

I nodded. "Yeah, I remember that. What does red mean?"

"Red means love."

"You're saying that you love me?" I asked.

"I'm saying that *you* love *me*."

I rolled my eyes. "Oh, wow. Chris, you're just too much."

He looked me in the eye and shook his head. "No, I'm just what you need."

When Raheem DeVaughn's "You" began to play, he opened the

door, stood next to the car, and reached for my hand. "Dance with me."

"Out here? On the parking lot?"

He nodded. "Yes, right here, right now."

I shrugged, thinking to myself that he was crazy and that anyone who saw us would think we were *both* crazy. I took his hand and let him pull me into his arms. With his phone sitting on the roof of his car providing the music, we danced beneath the stars on the hospital parking lot. I closed my eyes and thought to myself that I loved the way his arms felt around me. Just like he said, I was a perfect fit—we were a perfect fit for each other.

I opened my eyes and looked up at his face. His eyes were closed as he mouthed the words to the song, and he looked *so handsome.* I reached up and gently caressed his cheek, letting my fingers fall to graze his neck. I wanted to kiss him so badly. I *always* wanted to kiss him. I couldn't get enough of him or his kisses or the feeling of his arms around me. *Was I in love with him?* If I wasn't, I definitely *wanted* to be, and the feeling of wanting to be in love was strange, almost foreign to me. I'd spent most of my adult life running away from that feeling.

He opened his eyes and grasped my hand as it traveled to his chest. He brought my hand to his lips and kissed it softly. Then he leaned forward and kissed my lips again. When we finally parted, it was well past the time for me to return to work. Chris walked me to the employee entrance and I glided into the ER with a smile on my face. Throughout the remainder of my shift, my thoughts were of Chris and his kisses. I couldn't wait to see him again.

~*~

I'd been in St. Louis for two-and-a-half months and had spent most of my time between two places: the hospital and Chris's apartment. I only had two more weeks left on my assignment and had just about decided to sign on for another three months. The thought of leaving St. Louis and Chris King seemed unreal to me. I was happier than I'd been in years. Actually, I don't think I'd ever been as happy as I was with Chris. But best of all, the feeling was mutual. He adored me just as much as, if not more than, I adored him.

We spent our time together laughing and talking and just getting to know each other more and more. Little by little, I became comfortable enough with him to talk about some of my past experiences, most of which I wasn't proud of. I even opened up and told him about my relationships with my parents and my ex.

One evening, while Chris and I were lounging in his living room watching TV, he asked, "Why did you get a divorce?"

"What?" I replied, caught a little off-guard.

"Why did you and your husband get a divorce?" he repeated.

"Oh… well, we really hadn't been getting along very well for a couple of years. I did everything I could to make it work. I really did. I never wanted a divorce because my parents' divorce had been so horrible, and it really affected me. I just didn't want that for Tiffany, you know?

"Well, anyway, I couldn't make it work alone. As hard as I fought, Tim's heart just wasn't in it. So one day, he told me that he didn't want to be married anymore. And just like that, he moved out of our house and in with his current wife… and my marriage was over."

He sat up and looked me in the eye. "That must've been hard for you to deal with. I know it had to hurt you."

I nodded. "It did, and for a long time, I really and truly despised him. But I came to realize that just like it takes two to make a marriage, it takes two to break one. We were too young. I didn't know how to be a wife and he definitely didn't know how to be a husband. Plus, I was just a teenager when I had our daughter, and she became the tie that bound our relationship *and* our marriage. You can't build a relationship on the fact that you have a kid together. It just won't work."

"And then you had to raise her as a single mother? I know that took some strength. I've been there. Those years I had Russ were hectic, but they were also the most fulfilling years of my life."

I smiled. "Yeah, well, Tim was around, but I really did most of the raising alone. But it was definitely worth it. I feel like Tiffany is my greatest achievement. She turned out really well despite the fact that I had no clue what I was doing when I was raising her."

He laughed. "Well, they don't come with a manual. I ran my phone bill way up calling my mama when I first had to take care of Russ on my own."

"Well, my parents were right there with me the whole time, and for the most part, that was my biggest problem."

He frowned. "What do you mean?"

I sighed. "My family puts the *dys* in dysfunctional. My parents divorced when I was, like, seven, and they still can't stand each other. The only thing they can agree on is what a screw-up I am."

Chris cocked his head to the side and gave me a curious look. "Now, you don't believe that, do you? They're your parents. I know they love you."

"I guess they do love me in some twisted way, but all I've ever heard from them is how I should've done *this* or I could've done *that*. Never a word about how well I *did* manage to do. They just never got over my getting pregnant as a teenager and all that went along with that. I try not to dwell on how they feel about me, but it's hard when your own family doesn't accept you. I was depressed for years trying to deal with that stuff—suicidal, even."

He grasped my hand in his and gave it a little squeeze. "I'm sorry things were like that for you, baby, I really am. But what you have to remember is that God accepts you, and so do I. I love you, Marli."

"I know God does, and I know I would never have made it this far without His love and… what did you just say?"

He smiled sweetly. "I said I love you."

"Um, I know you kind of hinted at that before, with the red rose, but are you serious? You *love* me?"

He nodded. "I really do."

"Are you… are you sure?"

"*Very* sure."

"Are you just trying to get me to stay here? I've already been considering it, so you don't have to say that if you don't mean it."

He leaned closer to me. "Now, I ain't above lying to keep you here, but I mean it, baby. I love you. I wanted to tell you when I gave you the rose, but I got cold feet."

"Well, I've been thinking that I love you, too, but I don't know. It seems too soon to be falling in love. Isn't it?" I rambled.

"I don't think it's too soon. I know what I feel for you, and I know it ain't just *like*."

I looked into his eyes and shook my head. "I've gotta be honest with you. I'm afraid, Chris. I'm afraid this won't work and I'm scared to death of being hurt again."

"I'm a little afraid, too. I've been hurt before, remember? I know how it feels. I promise not to hurt you. Give me your heart. You can trust me with it."

"Really?"

"Have I given you any reason *not* to trust me?"

I dropped my eyes. "No. It's just that I've had my guard up for a long time. But you… you make me feel so… so—"

He reached over and pulled my face toward his. "I know. You make me feel the same way. All I wanna do is love you. That's it. No more, no less."

"I want you to love me. I wanna love you, too."

"Then go right ahead. I don't mind."

He kissed me softly on the lips. I leaned against him and closed my eyes. "Chris, I need to tell you something."

He gently rubbed my back. "What is it, baby?"

"It's… it's about my past. I hope it doesn't change how you feel about me."

He backed away a little and gave me a concerned look. "Nothing could change the way I feel about you, Marli."

I nodded. "O... okay. I... uh... after my divorce, I was really upset and I didn't really have anyone to talk to except for Carla, and I had a hard time coping. And I... I slept around a lot."

Chris raised an eyebrow. "Oh... well, I never said I was Saint Chris or nothing. I ain't no virgin, Marli."

"Um, Chris, I did some crazy stuff. Tiff was just a little girl back then, and sometimes I would wait until she went to sleep and leave her home alone and meet men at hotels. Half the time I didn't even know these men. I'd meet them in the grocery store or at the gas station and give them my number, and then we'd hook up."

Chris dropped his eyes and shook his head. "Damn..."

"I know."

His eyes met mine. "Why? Why would you do that? You're worth so much more than that."

"I don't know, I mean, I put all I had into my marriage and it tore me up when it fell apart. I... I guess I thought it would be easier to sleep around than try to have a real relationship with someone. I just didn't wanna get hurt again."

"What made you stop? I mean, you *have* stopped, right?"

"Yes, I have. Um, early one morning I came home and Tiffany was standing in the middle of the living room crying. She'd woken up in the middle of the night and was scared when she realized I was gone. After that, I slowed down a lot. Before I came here, I was down to one guy I'd see a couple of times a week."

Chris leaned forward and fixed his eyes on the floor. "What happened to him?" he asked softly.

"He was killed a few months ago. He was a drug dealer."

Chris glanced at me. "Man, that's messed up." He hesitated. "Um... Marli, have you been tested?"

"Yes, and since I did have sense enough to use condoms, I'm disease free."

"Me, too."

"Good."

He reached for my hand and grasped it in his. "This is in your past, right? It's over?"

"Yes. I haven't done anything like that since I've been here. Haven't wanted to, either."

He smiled. "I got something to do with that?"

"You have *everything* to do with it."

He leaned in and kissed me softly. "That's good to know. Look, the past is the past. And as long as I live, I plan to make your future much better than you could ever dream, baby. I love you, Marli. I really do. You don't ever have to wonder about that."

He hugged me and I relaxed in his embrace. "I love you, too, Chris."

FIFTEEN

"NO ORDINARY LOVE"

It was an odd off day for me in that I actually felt full of energy and was more than ready to get out and hit the streets of St. Louis with Chris. I didn't even let it bother me that Carla had slipped out of the apartment before dawn without a word.

I hopped out of bed, showered and dressed, and waited for Chris to call me just as he did every day. But as the day wore on, my phone didn't ring even once. I sat there in the living room and stared at it for the better part of the day and still no call. That afternoon, I finally called him—no answer, straight to voicemail. Now I was getting worried. Since we'd been seeing each other, he had never missed calling me.

And then a sinking feeling began to overtake me and with it, a rush of gloomy thoughts. *Maybe, it's over. He was bound to get sick of me. Who was I fooling, thinking he really loved me? I knew I shouldn't have gotten involved with him. It would've never worked, anyway. I knew it was too good to be true.*

I'd been wound up so tightly all day that I hadn't eaten a bite since nibbling on a piece of toast that morning. So I ordered a pizza and poured myself a soda to drown my sorrows in while I waited for my dinner to be delivered.

Thirty minutes later, I heard a knock at the door. I checked the peep hole expecting to see someone in a pizza uniform. Instead, I saw Chris King wearing a tuxedo. I stood there for a moment and debated whether or not to open the door. But then curiosity got the best of me. I needed to know why he was at my door at seven in the evening dressed like he was ready for a prom. And I also wanted to cuss him out for ignoring my call.

I opened the door and walked back into the apartment without bothering to greet him.

He trailed me into the living room. I plopped down on the sofa and crossed my arms at my chest.

He took a seat next to me. "You got a nice dress you can change into?"

"Why?" I asked angrily.

"Cause we got somewhere to be in an hour."

"I'm not going anywhere with you, Chris."

He frowned. "Why?"

My mouth fell open. "*Why?* Where have you been? Why didn't you call me? Why didn't you answer when I called *you*?"

A smile slowly spread across his face. "You're mad at me? You are so cute when you're mad."

I rolled my eyes. "*Answer me*, Chris."

"I was very busy today. I have a surprise for you. Can you go put on a dress for me?"

"Busy with what?"

"You'll see."

I continued to sit there. I wanted to stay mad at him, but I honestly couldn't. The man looked and smelled like heaven. But nevertheless, I sat there with my arms crossed and fought back the relieved smile that threatened to reveal itself.

"I'm sorry for neglecting you, but I promise to make up for it." He leaned close to me and kissed my cheek. "Please forgive me," he whispered in my ear. He planted another, feather-light kiss on my neck. "Pretty please." He moved the collar of my shirt and gently kissed my shoulder. "Pretty, pretty please, Mean Marli."

If I sat there any longer, I was either going to melt or explode or both. So I stood to my feet. "Fine. Give me a few minutes to change and everything."

He grinned up at me. "Thank you, baby."

I took a quick shower, made up my face, picked out my hair, and pulled on a red dress that I'd never worn before. I wasn't even sure why I'd brought it with me until that moment. As I inspected myself in the mirror, I had to admit that I looked nice. Not as nice or formal as Chris in his tux, but my look complemented his fairly well.

I slipped on a pair of black pumps, and as I stepped back into the living room, Chris stood to his feet and clutched his chest over his heart. "Dang, baby. You just took my breath away. You look *gorgeous*."

I walked over to him and he pulled me into his arms. "No, I don't look half as gorgeous as you do," I said.

He looked into my eyes. "You'll be the most beautiful woman in the place."

"What place?"

"Like I said, it's a surprise."

I glanced at the coffee table and noticed a pizza box. "I see my dinner arrived."

"Yeah, but what I have in mind will beat pizza any day."

"Mm-hmm," I said as I followed him out of my apartment. "We'll see."

A few minutes later, we were riding through the streets of St. Louis on our way to Chris's surprise. I felt stupid for being angry with him, for believing he had ignored me. It was becoming more and more evident to me just how much my past experiences had screwed up my mind. Chris had never given me any reason to believe he was anything but a stand-up guy. My little meltdown earlier had been more about me than him.

Chris parked his car and led me to the doors of a place that was very familiar to me—Charmaine's. I smiled as I followed him inside, but as we entered the club, I found it to be uncharacteristically empty.

Puzzled, I leaned close to Chris as we navigated our way through the empty space. "Are we the first ones here?" I whispered.

He grinned down at me. "You could say that."

We sat at the same table my friends and I had shared the first time I ever laid eyes on Chris King. We ordered drinks and engaged in light conversation. We'd been there about fifteen minutes when the MC took the stage. We were still the only patrons in the club.

"Good evening, *lady* and *gentleman*. Tonight we have a special treat for you. A St. Louis favorite! Presenting, *all* The St. Louis Kingsmen!"

I glanced around the room and lightly clapped my hands as the band began to take the stage. "Be back in a bit," Chris said and then joined the band.

I was confused and happy at the same time. I loved listening to the band and watching them perform, but what was going on? Where was everyone else?

I watched as Chris grabbed the microphone, his eyes fixed on me.

"Marli Meadows, this show is for you. I love you, baby. Enjoy."

And so I sat there with a permanent smile on my face as Chris King and The St. Louis Kingsmen serenaded me. They sounded wonderful, giving little old me the full effects of their talents. They held nothing back as Quinton Farver blessed me with his voice and Chris and the other bandmates backed him up.

I felt special—no, I felt *loved* as Chris played his trumpet with his eyes glued to mine. And I felt nothing but love for him in return.

When the band began to play "Your Love Is King," I closed my eyes and swayed in my chair. About halfway through the song, I felt someone place their hand gently on my shoulder. I opened my eyes to see that Chris had abandoned his post on stage and was standing next to me. He offered me his hand and said, "May I have this dance, lovely lady?"

The band continued to play an absolutely beautiful version of the song as I took his hand and we stepped onto the spotless dance floor. Chris smiled down at me. "Are you enjoying yourself?"

I returned his smile. I don't think I'd ever smiled that much in such a short amount of time. "Absolutely."

"More than you would've enjoyed that pizza?"

I giggled. "Yes, *much* more. I'm sorry for the attitude I gave you earlier. If I'd known this was what you were up to all day…"

"Then it wouldn't have been a surprise." He pulled me closer to him.

I breathed in his scent and sighed. "Thank you, Chris. No one has ever, *ever* done anything like this for me before."

"Well, then you been keeping the wrong company, baby. You deserve this and more. And if you let me, I'ma give it to you."

I closed my eyes, still wearing a smile that someone would have to break my face to remove. "Hmm, I look forward to it."

Chris relaxed his hold on me and when I opened his eyes, I found his gaze fixed on my face. He leaned in close enough for our lips to barely touch. "I love you, baby," he said, huskily.

"I love you, too, Chris."

Then his lips met mine. He held my face in his hands and kissed me through the end of the song and the beginning of another. And then he embraced me and we danced until we'd danced the night away. I never wanted that night to end.

~*~

I kissed Chris on the cheek then left the living room of my apartment and headed to my bedroom to get ready for work. I'd finished my three months and was beginning a new, six-month contract with the hospital. Carla had opted to stay for another three months, leaving her kids with her ex back in Arkansas. Her behavior had become so erratic that when he wasn't out of town with the band, Chris took me to work. It was the only way I knew I'd get there on time.

As I undressed and headed out of the room to the shower, my cell phone began to ring. I was surprised to see Tiffany's number pop up on the screen. Except for the occasional text message, I'd barely heard from her in the past three months.

I plopped down on the side of the bed. "Hello?"

"Hey, Mama!" Tiffany chirped.

I smiled. "Well, hello, Ms. Meadows. Long time no hear."

She laughed. "I'm sorry, but I've really been busy. There's always something to do here, and I've made so many friends."

"That's good. I'm glad you've adjusted so well. I knew you'd love it."

"I do! So how are you? How's St. Louis?"

"St. Louis is good—no, *great*. Oh, and if you wanna see me for the holidays, you'll have to come to St. Louis. I'm staying a while longer."

"Really? You must *really* like it there. Have *you* made any new friends?"

My smile widened. "Well, yeah, I have. Um, there's one in particular that I'd like for you to meet. His name's Chris."

"Is this Chris the reason for your extended stay in St. Louis?"

"Well, he definitely has something to do with it. He's a great person. I think you'll like him."

"I'm happy for you, Mama. I've always wished you could find some real happiness. You know? I can hear how happy you are. It's all in your voice."

"I *am* happy, Tiff. I'm actually thinking about moving here permanently."

"I think you should."

"Really, Tiff?"

"Yeah. There's nothing back home but bad memories. If you're happy there, why not stay?"

I walked over to the door and closed it.

"Um, there's something I need to tell you about Chris," I whispered into the phone.

"What is it?" she asked, sounding concerned.

"Well, uh… he's white."

"Oh, is that all? I thought he was a murderer or an ex-con or something."

"So you're okay with him being white?"

"Well, *is* he an ex-con or a murderer?"

"No! He's a musician, a preacher's son."

"Oh, well, then yeah, I'm okay with it. It wouldn't matter to me if he was black, white, green, or red. As long as he treats you right, we'll get along fine."

I nodded as if she could see me through the phone. "He treats me like a queen."

"Then he gets my approval."

"Thanks, Tiff. That means a lot to me."

"Hey, Mom, there's one thing I need to say to you."

"Okay."

"If you care about him and he's good to you, then you don't need anyone's approval to be with him. Not even mine. It's your life, Mama. Live it for yourself."

"Well, well, who exactly is the mother here?" I asked.

"Look, a person doesn't have to have a baby to know some things. Well, I gotta go. I'll talk to you soon, I promise. I love you, Mama."

"I love you, too, Tiff, and I owe you an apology."

"For what?"

"All these years, I let my folks interfere with how I raised you. I even let them make some decisions I should've made for you or helped you to make. I never even asked you if you really wanted to go to Spelman."

"Aw, Mama. You did the best you could."

"I guess so, but let me say this—if that's not the school you chose for yourself and if law is not the career path for you, then change it. I'll respect whatever you choose to do with your life."

"Thank you, Mama. I really needed to hear that."

"You're welcome. Bye, sweetie."

"Bye, Mama."

I ended the call and headed down the hall to the shower, smiling all the while. Yeah, I have to say, at that point, I was pretty happy.

SIXTEEN

"NOTHING CAN COME BETWEEN US"

I walked into the kitchen and nearly jumped out of my skin when I saw Carla sitting at the table. I assumed she still lived in the apartment with me, but we hadn't crossed paths in more than two weeks. I eyed her cautiously as I walked over to the refrigerator.

"Good morning," she said softly.

I stopped in my tracks and turned around to look at her. Something in her voice didn't sound right. Sure enough, I could see that her face was wet with tears. "Carla, are you okay?" I asked as I walked over and took a seat at the table.

She laughed bitterly. "No, I'm definitely *not* okay. What are you doing up so early on an off day? I figured it'd be a while before you woke up."

"Um, Chris and I are gonna drive to Pine Bluff to pick up my car. Carla, what's wrong?"

"Chris, huh? Must be love 'cuz you're glowing."

I smiled. "Yeah, it's love. Um… Carla, tell me what's the matter with you."

She sighed and shook her head. "I guess I've been running around here with all these guys, occupying my mind, and suddenly this morning, I woke up alone for the first time in weeks. It was too quiet, too still, and my mind started reeling."

"You started thinking about things back home?"

A tear rolled down her cheek as she nodded. "Yeah. You know, Marli, I thought I had it all together. I thought my life was pretty good and I never, *ever* would've thought Bryan would cheat on me. I mean, we had the house, the cars, the good jobs, great kids. When I found out he was cheating on me, I couldn't believe it. I was *devastated*."

"You *know* I understand how you feel, but there's just no way to predict if a man will cheat or not, Carla. You just have to pray for your marriage and your family. I believe y'all can still work it out."

She shook her head. "Too much has happened now. I hate to tell you how many guys I've been with since we've been here. And what Bryan did is just unforgiveable. It's over, Marli. My marriage is over, and my family is destroyed."

I leaned forward and grabbed her hand. "Listen, Carla. Do you still love Bryan?"

She wiped a tear from her cheek. "Marli, it's not that simple. If me loving him could fix things, we would've reconciled months ago."

"What's so complicated? You love him, and I'm sure he loves you. You two just have to forgive each other and *make* things work."

"It's not that simple! It's over, Marli. There's nothing that can save my marriage. It's... it's *unfixable*."

I frowned. "Look, Carla. Nothing's so broken that it can't be fixed. You just have to try."

She sighed. "You remember I told you I caught Bryan with someone from our church?"

"Yeah, but that doesn't make a difference. You can still work things out."

"It was a man."

"Huh, what? Who was a man?"

"I caught him in our bed with *another man*—one of the deacons. Now, how we gonna fix *that*, Marli? Tell me how?!" Carla jumped up from her chair and began pacing the floor.

"Um, well... Carla, I... I don't...." My voice trailed off because I honestly didn't know what to say.

"Uh-huh, *exactly*. You're speechless, huh? Imagine how I felt walking into my own house, my own *bedroom*, and finding my husband, the damn love of my life, in bed with another man! How can we fix things when I'm obviously not what Bryan wants?!"

I cleared my throat. "Did... did Bryan say that he was gay or bisexual?"

She laughed bitterly and shook her head. "Of course not. He said he was just experimenting. He said that that was his first and last time with a man. As if I can believe *that*."

"Well, maybe it's the truth. How can you say it's a lie?"

"It doesn't matter if it's the truth or a lie, Marli! The fact is that he did it. I *saw* him doing it. Do you understand how that made me feel as a woman? That's why I've been wilding out since we got here. I... I just needed to feel wanted. I wanted to feel like I was enough for someone. *Anyone*."

I stood and placed my hand on Carla's shoulder. "Carla, you're a beautiful, smart woman. You can't make what Bryan did be about you. It's about him and whatever he's got going on inside of him. It doesn't mean you're undesirable as a woman."

Carla slumped back into her chair. "But it *does* mean that I wasn't enough for him. I mean, had it been a woman, maybe I could've competed. I can't compete with a man. No sense in trying."

I shook my head. "It's not about competing. Carla, you need to pray. Pray for healing and for restoration."

She looked up at me, her eyes filled with tears. "The restoration and healing of my marriage? How's that possible?"

"Not necessarily your marriage. Pray for the restoration of your hope and the healing of your heart. You can't decide that what Bryan did is some unpardonable sin, Carla. It's not for you to judge and determine that. It's your responsibility to forgive him."

"And then what? Act like it didn't happen and hope it won't happen again?"

I lowered my eyes. "I can't answer that. I don't have all the answers. But I do know that nothing's impossible with God. He can heal and restore your marriage if that's His will, or He can heal and restore you and give you the strength to go on and raise your sons as a single mother. Just know that whatever you need, He's got it."

She nodded. "Yeah, you're right. I *know* you're right. It's just hard to see that when your vision is blinded by so much pain. And anyway, when did you get so spiritual?"

"I'm not a *total* heathen, Carla. Plus, I've learned a lot from Chris's dad during his sermons every Sunday and from Chris, himself. Chris studies the Bible every night. Prays all the time. He's a good influence."

She smiled and sniffled. "I'm sorry, Marli. I've been acting such a fool. If I were you, I probably wouldn't even talk to me anymore."

"I love you, Carla, and you'll always be my girl. Just remind me to never share living quarters with you again. You're a *lousy* roommate."

She laughed. "Yeah, I am. So… are you moving in with Chris?"

I shook my head. "Naw, he's too good a guy for me to be shacking up with. I wanna do things right with him. I have more than enough experience with doing things the wrong way."

"That's smart of you. So… uh, are you two getting serious?"

I nodded. "We're definitely getting closer. Carla, he's sweet and kind, and he's so good to me. I never thought I could be this happy with *anyone*."

"So you finally got over him being white? He's not *Justin Timberfake* anymore, huh?"

I laughed. "Funny thing is, the more I got to know him, the more his color didn't matter. He's just Chris to me now, and he's wonderful. I think I could see us having a future together."

"I'm really happy for you, Marli. If anyone deserves to be happy, it's you."

"Thanks, Carla."

A knock at the door interrupted our conversation. "That must be Chris now," I said.

"All right, y'all have a safe trip. I'ma go and pray now and try to piece my life back together."

"Sounds like a good plan. I'll be praying for you. I'll talk to you later."

"Okay."

Minutes later, Chris and I were walking across the parking lot to his car. When he stopped at a shiny, black Lincoln Navigator, I frowned.

"You rented this for the trip? Chris, you didn't have to do that. The rate must be outrageous!"

He smiled. "Uh, no… I bought it yesterday. I thought it would be a more comfortable ride."

"Um, Chris? You're saying you bought this truck yesterday? Are you taking it back or something?"

He laughed. "No, baby. I *bought* it. It's mine."

"Chris, this is like a fifty-thousand-dollar vehicle. Your note must be ridiculous! Are you sure you can afford this? Is the Mercedes paid off, or did you trade it in or something?"

He opened the door for me. "Thanks for being concerned about me, but I'm fine. I can afford it."

I climbed into the huge SUV and fastened my seatbelt. I *was* concerned. How could Chris possibly afford all of this? Was he into something he didn't want me to know about? I was sure my worry was written all over my face when he climbed into the driver's seat.

He leaned over and kissed me. "Ah, stop worrying. It's all right, baby. I got some money saved up. I'm not breaking myself."

I nodded then turned and looked him in the eye. "Uh-huh. Chris, are you selling drugs or something?"

He threw his head back and laughed. "Come on, Marli. You know I'm not a drug dealer. I'm a preacher's kid, remember?"

"Well, I'm just trying to figure out how you can afford all this stuff. The band can't be making *that* much. Y'all only perform a couple of nights a week. Plus you have to split the money. I love you, but I don't want to be in the middle of anything illegal. You know my past. I know what the end result of that life can be and I don't think I could stand it if something happened to you."

He leaned closer to me and rubbed my neck with his fingertip. "Baby, nothing's gonna happen to me because I'm not doing anything illegal. I got some money saved up, that's all."

I sighed. "You wouldn't lie to me, would you?"

He shook his head. "I promise you, I am telling the truth. I bought everything I have with legal money. I'm strictly legit."

"Okay," I said and then rubbed my finger across the diamond and silver cross that hung from my necklace. It had been a gift from Chris a few days earlier, and I'd thought it was pretty expensive.

"*Everything*, including that necklace," he said.

I nodded and then peered out the window as we pulled out of the parking lot.

~*~

About five hours later, we arrived in Little Rock, Arkansas. Chris exited the highway on the outskirts of town, pulled into a gas station, and handed me money for the gas. I went inside to pay for the gas and when I made it back to the truck, Chris was holding my phone in his hand.

"You checking up on me?" I asked playfully.

"No, I was calling your dad."

"What?!" I nearly yelled. I snatched the phone from him. "Why on earth would you do that?!"

"Because I wanna meet him. He says he's at home right now."

I shook my head vigorously. "No, no, *no*, Chris. *No way*. It'll be a disaster. I'm telling you, nothing good will come of this."

"Come on, Marli. He's your father. You've met my parents. I wanna meet yours."

I was on the edge of a full-on panic attack. "Please don't do this. *Please.* I'm telling you—you *don't* wanna do this. He won't accept you and there's no telling what he'll say to you."

Chris frowned slightly. "Why? Because I'm white?"

"Because you're white or because you're tall or a musician or you're right handed. It doesn't matter who or what you are. If you're with me, he *won't* accept you."

"If he doesn't accept me, will it change the way *you* feel about me?"

I looked at him and shook my head again. "Of course not."

"Then let me meet him. I can handle rejection. I'm a big boy."

"You have no idea what you're asking."

"Yeah, I do. What's the address?"

I sucked in a breath and looked out the window.

"Come on, Marli. Please give me the address, or tell me how to get there or something."

I leaned back against the seat and placed my hand on my forehead. "Okay, fine. We can go to my father's house. We'll get there before we get to Pine Bluff. Get back on the highway. I'll tell you how to get there."

Twenty minutes later, we were pulling onto the driveway in front of my father's home. Chris opened the door for me, and I slid out of the truck with a drawn look on my face.

"Dang, Marli. You look like you're headed for the electric chair,"

Chris said as I took his hand and led him up the steps to the front door.

"I am," I muttered.

Before he could reply, the door swung open to reveal Carmen on the other side. "Marli! Your dad said you were on your way over with a friend." She looked up at Chris. "Oh, I see. Well, come on in."

"Um, Carmen, this is Chris King. Chris, this is my father's wife, Carmen."

As we walked into the house, Chris shook Carmen's hand. "Nice to meet you, Mrs. White."

Carmen's eyes widened as Chris spoke. "Um, well, the pleasure's all mine."

Chris and I followed her into the den where my father was seated on the sofa. As we rounded the corner, he looked up and smiled, then, upon seeing Chris, the smile began to fade. *Here it comes*, I thought.

"Honey, Marli and her friend are here," Carmen announced as she took a seat next to my father.

My father stood to his feet. "Well, I can see that, dear." He looked at me. "Marli, aren't you going to introduce me to your friend?"

"Um... yes, sir. Daddy, this is Chris King. Chris, this is my father, Marlon White."

My father grasped Chris's hand. "*Attorney* Marlon White."

"Good to meet you, sir. Marli's told me a lot about you."

"Well, good. You two have a seat."

Chris and I each sat in one of the matching, leather wingback chairs that were situated opposite the couch. I glanced at Chris and he flashed that brilliant smile of his. On any other occasion, his smile would have lifted my mood, but instead, I felt worse. I knew that by the time we left my father's house, Chris's smile would be long gone.

"So, Marli, how's St. Louis been?" my father asked.

I leaned back in the chair and clasped my hands in my lap. "Actually, it's been nice. I've extended my contract."

"I see. And Chris, what do you do for a living?"

"I'm a musician, sir. I play the trumpet, and I manage my own band."

"Hip hop?" my father asked.

"No, sir. Jazz and R&B."

"What's the name of your band?"

"The St. Louis Kingsmen."

"Hmm, never heard of them."

"Well, no, sir. We're pretty popular in St. Louis and Chicago. We travel a little bit, but we're not real famous yet."

"You must be doing pretty well. That's a nice vehicle you have, Chris," Carmen said.

Chris smiled. "Yes, ma'am. We do okay."

"I see," my father said. "So you and Marli are friends?"

"Well, actually, we're seeing each other, sir. I care a lot about Marli. I *love* her."

My father raised his eyebrows. "Really? And how does Marli feel about you?"

Chris smiled at me. "Well, she can answer that, sir."

"I, uh, feel the same way about him. I-I love him, too," I stammered.

"I see. Marli, have you met Chris's family?" my father inquired.

I smiled. "Yes, I have. They're really good people." I knew where my father was trying to go with that question. He had no idea how far up the wrong tree he was barking.

"So... Chris, your parents are accepting of you dating black women?" my father asked.

Chris gave me a knowing look. "Oh, yes, sir. They're happy as long as I'm happy, and I'm *very* happy with Marli."

"Mm-hmm," my father said and then turned to me. "Marli, I'd like to speak to Chris alone for a moment. Can you leave us?"

I flashed Chris a panicked look. I knew there was no way I should leave him alone with my father. He'd eat him alive.

Chris smiled at me and nodded. I was sure that Chris's inflated confidence combined with my father's evilness would equal the end of my relationship with Chris. I sat there for a moment, trying to decide whether or not I should just grab Chris's hand and run out of the house.

Chris stood to his feet and moved closer to my chair. He bent over and kissed me on my cheek. "Go on, baby," he whispered. "It'll be okay."

I looked up at him and then over at my father, who looked like he was about to blow a gasket at the sight of Chris kissing me. I nodded, and as I stood to leave, looked over at Carmen who hadn't moved a muscle. I guess my father's request didn't apply to her.

Chris took my hand and gave it a reassuring squeeze, and I left the room and walked into the kitchen. I stood behind the door and listened to their conversation.

"Chris, let me be honest with you. I'm a little confused about this situation," my father said.

"Sir?" Chris said, sounding confused himself.

"What are you doing here with my daughter?"

"I'm not exactly sure what you mean, sir."

"Okay, let me be blunt with you. You're a nice-looking guy. A nice-looking *white* guy. I'm sure you could have your pick of women—black or white. What are you doing with Marli?"

"Well, like I said, I care for her. I'm in love with her."

"Son, what is it that you want here? What are you after? Marli doesn't have any access to any money. She's just a nurse. Now, *I* have money, but I'm not in the business of giving it away."

"What?!" Chris said, sounding even more confused.

"Well, you come here with Marli, sounding and dressed like a black man. What are you? Some kind of rapper? Thought you could use my money to start your career?"

"With all due respect, sir, I don't need *anyone's* money. Least of all, yours. I'm here because I love your daughter."

"Are you gonna sit there and tell me that you love someone like Marli? I can't see how that's possible."

"What does that mean?" Chris was beginning to raise his voice. As cool and calm as he was, I could tell my father was getting under his skin.

I grabbed the doorknob but then decided to wait.

"How can you be in love with a woman her size? Okay, so maybe you like black women, but *fat* black women?"

"Sir, your daughter is *exactly* the kind of woman I like. I love *everything* about her. I actually came here today to ask for her hand in marriage."

At that point I think I forgot I was eavesdropping. I swung the kitchen door open and stepped back into the den.

"What?!" my father and I said simultaneously.

Chris stood and walked over to me. "I love you, Marli, and I wanna marry you."

Before I could reply, my father said, "What?! How are you gonna take care of her? Oh, that's right. She's a nurse, so you're gonna live off of her."

Chris turned to my father with a serious look on his face. "Sir, I can guarantee you that I don't have to live off of Marli. I'm more than capable of taking care of her. She could quit her job today if she wanted to."

"Sure she could," my father said sarcastically. "Well, what if I don't give you my blessing?"

Chris turned back to me. "Then I'll pray for God to soften your heart, and if Marli will still have me, I'ma marry her anyway. I just hope you change your mind so you can be in our children's lives."

"*Children?* You two won't last long enough for that. Or is she already pregnant? Is that what this is all about?"

"No! *I'm not!* Come on, now. Does it always have to be that I've messed up?" I finally said.

"Is it really that hard for you to believe that I love her and that I want to be with her?" Chris asked.

"I don't understand how you could," my father replied.

Chris nodded. "Well, I've said what I came here to say." He turned to Carmen. "It was nice meeting you, Mrs. White."

Carmen smiled and nodded but didn't say a word.

Chris grabbed my hand. I looked up at him and shook my head in disgust. He gave me an apologetic look.

"You ready to go?" he asked softly.

I nodded.

Chris turned his attention back to my father. "Well, you all have a good rest of the day. I'll keep you in my prayers."

My father just sat there and stared at us. After a few seconds of awkward silence, Carmen stood and walked over to us.

"Let me show you two out," she offered.

We'd turned to leave when my father spoke again. "Marli, I certainly hope you didn't think he would impress me just because he's white." That was it. I'd hit my limit with him.

I turned to him with disgust written all over my face. "Daddy, I'm a grown woman. I'm not here looking for your approval, because I don't need it. Chris wanted to meet you, and that's why we're here—not because I was delusional enough to think you'd accept him and not because I *need* you to accept him. *I* accept him and I love him, and most importantly, *he* loves *me*. No matter how low *your* opinion of me may be, *he* loves me for who I am. Every word that comes out of your mouth shows me that you really don't know me at all, and that makes me sad for *you*." I turned to Carmen and added, "I know the way out."

My heart was racing as I gripped Chris's hand tightly and led him to front door. Once we were outside the house and inside of Chris's truck, he said, "I'm sorry I put you through that, but my intentions were pure, you know?"

I nodded. "I know. Uh, Chris, did you really mean what you said about marrying me?"

"Yes, baby. Look, I didn't drive you here just to pick up your car. Shoot, you don't even need it—you can drive one of mine. We can still pick up the car, but the real reason I drove you here was to ask for your hand in marriage." He opened the center console, reached inside, and pulled out a ring box. I clasped my hand over my mouth and looked from the ring box to his face.

I let out a muffled, "Oh."

Chris opened the box to reveal an absolutely gorgeous ring.

"Oh, Chris, it's beautiful!" I whispered as I stared at it.

"Well, will you accept it? Will you marry me?"

"But we've only known each other for a couple of months. Don't you think this is a little fast?" I asked—my eyes still glued to the ring. I think my mouth started to water.

He shook his head. "No. Look, baby, later ain't promised to us. We don't need to wait. I wanna love you and make you my wife as soon as I can. I want my happily ever after *right now*."

I dropped my eyes. "Chris, I'm scared."

Chris leaned in closer to me and kissed me softly. "I love you, Marli. I love you and I want to marry you. You don't have any reason to be scared. I'm *not* gonna hurt you, baby. I'd never, *ever* hurt you. You can count on that."

I looked from his face to the ring and shook my head.

"Listen, baby. There's one thing I'm sure of: this is meant to be. *We're* meant to be. I prayed for this—*for you*. I was so lonely before you. I just wanted something real. I prayed and prayed and then there you were, sitting in front of the stage looking so beautiful. It was like there was a spotlight on you. And I could hear God saying, 'There she is. I made her just for you.' So I sent you that drink and tried to work my magic on you."

I smiled.

"When you rejected me, I thought maybe I was wrong about you. But then I saw you at the hospital that day looking beautiful and exhausted, and I knew I was right. God put you at that table in front of the stage that night, and then he put you in front of the ER that morning. He even led you to my father's church. God orchestrated this whole thing. You are the answer to my prayers. I believe that whole-heartedly. We love each other, Marli. *Marry me.*"

I looked up at his face and remembered Tiffany's words. "*Live your life for yourself.*" Chris loved me, I loved him, and I was happy with him. With him, I was truly living for the first time in my life. I honestly couldn't think of one valid reason *not* to marry him.

"Okay," I said.

"Okay?" he repeated.

"Okay, yes, I'll marry you."

Chris's smile grew so wide, I was afraid he'd break his face. I smiled as he slid the ring onto my finger.

"Thank you, baby," he said and then leaned in and kissed me. "I love you so much."

"I love you, too."

As he pulled the SUV out of my father's driveway, I asked, "When are you gonna tell your parents?"

"I already did and my mother is expecting some grandchildren ASAP."

"So you told them we were getting married before you even asked me?"

He nodded. "Yep. I knew you'd say yes."

I shook my head. "Do you ever think that maybe you're a little overconfident?"

"Well, you *did* say yes, didn't you? I know you, Marli. I know you from head to toe and from soul to spirit. You love me, and I'm exactly what you need in your life."

I raised my eyebrows. "Really now? You think so?"

He stopped the car at the edge of the driveway, leaned across the console, and kissed me deeply. "I know so, baby."

"Maybe I'm what *you* need in *your* life, Chris. You ever think of it that way?"

"I know you are. With you by my side, I know I can do anything. Shoot, I could be the next black president if I wanted to. It'd be Bill, Barack, and Chris."

I laughed. "You're the blackest of the three by far."

He grinned. "And you know this."

I smiled and looked out the window as we left my father's

property. For the first time, my father's words hadn't broken me down. More than anything, I felt bad for him. My life was heading in a wonderful direction, and he'd miss it all.

SEVENTEEN

"BY YOUR SIDE"

Chris pulled into the driveway next to my house in Pine Bluff and parked behind my car.

"I hope it'll start," I said as I unlocked the front door.

Chris placed his hand on my shoulder and gently rubbed it. "We'll see in the morning."

We planned to spend the night at my house and head back to St. Louis in the morning. One six-hour drive was enough for me for one day. We walked inside to find my house undisturbed and everything in its place. I went into the kitchen to get some plates for the barbeque dinners we'd bought in town and strode back into the living room to find Chris standing in front of the mantle, looking at some of my family photos.

He picked up Tiffany's prom picture. "So this is Tiffany, huh?"

I nodded. "Yep, the one and only Tiffany Meadows."

He smiled. "She's a beautiful girl. Almost as beautiful as her mother."

"Well, thank you. That's the first time I've heard that one."

"Really? I mean it. You're the most beautiful girl in the world to me." He smiled at me and then rested his hand on my cheek.

I looked into his eyes. "I... I wish I could see what you see when you look at me."

Chris frowned. "Oh, baby. You don't see it? You got a mirror in here somewhere?"

I nodded and led him to my bedroom where we stood in front of the dresser mirror.

Chris stood behind me and rested his hands on my shoulders. "Look at those eyes. Beautiful brown eyes that hold so much sadness sometimes, I just want to kiss your pain away. And those lips, so full and soft." He turned me around and kissed me.

I smiled. "Hmm."

He gently caressed my neck. "Your skin, so smooth." His eyes surveyed my body. "And those curves. Thank *God* for those curves. And if you turn around right now, the rear view will literally make me lose my mind."

I rolled my eyes. "Whatever, Chris. You are so crazy."

He pulled me into a warm hug. "Crazy about you, baby."

I sighed. "I'm crazy about you, too."

We returned to the living room, settled down on the sofa, and ate our dinner and afterward, I leaned my head on Chris's shoulder as we listened to some music on the radio.

"I'm sorry about the things your dad said earlier," he said as he held my hand.

I sighed. "*You* didn't say them, and believe it or not, I'm used to it. He has a certain opinion of what's acceptable to him, and I'm just not it. I'm either too much of this or not enough of that in his eyes."

Chris looked down at me and rubbed my cheek with his fingertip. "Has it always been that way between the two of you?"

"Yeah, but this is the first time I've ever defended myself."

"Really? How do you feel about that?"

"I feel good. It was long overdue. I feel like I'm finally taking control of my life, of my happiness."

"*Are* you happy?"

"I am. Being with you—being *loved* by you—makes me very, very happy."

"Good. You know what would make me very, very happy?"

I smiled. "Hmm, what?"

"If I could meet your mother."

I shook my head. "Chris, *no*."

He sat up and looked me in the eye. "Come on. If we're gonna get married, I need to meet your family."

"Chris, if you keep meeting my family, you're gonna back out of marrying me."

"No, I won't. I'm still here, aren't I?"

"I'll tell you now, my mother thinks she can say anything she wants, and she's pretty opinionated."

"Didn't I just meet her in the form of your father? I can handle it. I don't break easily."

Well, he *had* held his own with my father.

I sighed. "Okay, let me call her. I guess we can have breakfast with her and my stepfather. Maybe if we go early enough, she'll still be sober."

Chris smiled and kissed my cheek. "Thank you, baby."

~*~

The next morning, we took my car, which started without a hitch, and drove to my mother's for breakfast. I'd told her I was bringing my new boyfriend with me, and she seemed pretty eager to meet Chris.

I knocked on her door and held my breath as we waited. It was Fred who answered the door.

"There she is!" he said cheerfully and pulled me into a tight hug. "You ran away, didn't you?"

I smiled. "Yeah, but I had to come back to see my favorite person."

"Oh, that's my girl." He reached over and shook Chris's hand. "This your guy?"

I nodded. "Mr. Fred, this is Chris King, my *fiancé*. Chris, this is my stepfather and the sweetest man in the world, Fred Gray."

"Fiancé? Well, then you're family!" Mr. Fred said and then lowered his voice. "Does your mama know yet?"

I shook my head. "Not yet."

"Well, come on in."

We followed him through the cluttered house, into the dining room where there was a huge array of food on the table. I looked up at Chris who mouthed "Wow."

"Edna!" Mr. Fred shouted, "They're here. Come on!"

Chris and I took our seats at the table. "Did you cook all of this, Mr. Fred?" I asked.

He nodded. "Yep. We got bacon, ham, scrambled eggs, grits, toast, pancakes, fried green tomatoes, and fried potatoes."

"Aw, man," Chris said excitedly. "This is great!"

I grinned. "Yeah, Mr. Fred is the best."

My mother finally made her entrance, dressed in a colorful caftan and gold slippers. "Well, hello!" she said. I couldn't readily tell if she was sober, but she appeared to be.

I stood and hugged her. "Hey, Mama, this is Chris, my fiancé."

"Fiancé!" she shrieked. "Well, congratulations!" She looked over at Chris and I think it finally registered with her that he was white. "Oh, uh, I'm Edna."

Chris flashed her a smile, then stood and shook her hand. "Nice to meet you, ma'am."

She nodded with a weird smile on her face. "Well, isn't this nice. Let's eat and I wanna hear all about how you two met."

Breakfast was actually nice, and my mother behaved herself, much to my surprise. She seemed to like Chris, but then again he *was* very likable. He was charming and full of personality, and my mother was always a sucker for a handsome man.

After breakfast, Fred took Chris out to the garage to show him his record collection, and my mother took me into the living room to grill me.

"So you're engaged, huh?" she asked.

"Yes, ma'am," I said with a smile.

"I can't believe you went to St. Louis and came back with a *white* man. To each his own, I guess."

"He's so good to me; I don't even see his color anymore. I just see his heart."

"Well, he's nice enough, and he seems to really care about you."

I nodded.

"You love him?"

"I do, and I truly believe he loves me, too."

"And he's a musician? You think you'll be okay for money?"

"Well, evidently so. Money hasn't been a problem for him so far. I haven't had to pay for so much as a Tic Tac since we've been together."

"Judging from that ring, he must have some good credit. That's a plus."

I nodded again.

"Well, that's good. How is he in bed?"

"Mama!"

She raised her eyebrows. "Well, is he any good? Don't act like that's not important."

I closed my eyes. I couldn't believe she was asking me that. "I wouldn't know."

"You haven't had sex with him?" she asked, as if the notion was absurd.

"No, I haven't."

"Why?"

"Mama, *really*?"

"I'm just saying, how are you gonna buy the car without first taking it for a test drive?"

"Um, isn't that the way things are supposed to go according to the Bible? He's a preacher's son, Mama. He wants to try to do things the right way, and so do I."

"Yeah, well, I did notice that he has some good equipment down there, and he talks and acts like a black man, so maybe he does other things like a black man." She was dead serious.

"You looked at his... his—"

She nodded. "Yep, I noticed that he has a nice package, so I think you'll be okay."

All I could do was shake my head. Leave it to my mother to notice the "important things."

About an hour later, my mother finally released us and gave me her blessing.

"That wasn't bad at all, and Mr. Fred is a real cool dude," Chris said as he backed my car out of my mother's driveway.

I nodded. "Yeah, he's always been great, and my mother's okay as long as she's sober."

"So, uh, what did your mother have to say about me?"

I laughed. "You really don't wanna know."

Chris glanced over at me. "Well, does she hate me, like me, or what?"

"Oh, my mother likes you. You're a man, and that's pretty much all that's required with her."

"Okay, I guess that's good. Well, what did she say?"

I covered my face with my hand. "Um, that you've got a nice package and that since you talk and act like a black man, you're probably good in bed."

"Ooooh. Um, so your mom's a freak?" he asked with raised eyebrows.

"Basically, yeah."

"Is that something you inherited from her? Because if it is, I'm definitely okay with that."

I shot him a sly smile. "I'm not telling. You'll just have to wait and see."

"Yeah, about that. I'm thinking we can go ahead and get married really soon. I'm trying to hold out here, but I ain't Superman."

"Um, so is that why you're marrying me? You tryna get me in bed."

He shook his head. "Naw, baby. I'm marrying you because I love you."

I leaned over and kissed him. "I love you, too."

"So I was thinking that you could go ahead and move your stuff into my place like next week, and we could be married right after that. Or we could do it today if you want to, 'cuz I'm ready."

"Wow, um, really? You don't want a wedding?"

"Not unless you want one. If you want one, we can have the biggest wedding in the world. But honestly, I don't need all that. I just wanna marry you and be with you."

"Well, okay then."

"Really?"

"Yeah."

He pulled my car into the driveway at my house and leaned over and kissed me. "I love you so much."

"Mm, I love you, too, Chris."

I walked around to the driver's side of the car and he leaned over and kissed me again.

"Oh, and by the way, there are some things I do even *better* than a black man." He winked and then headed off to his truck.

I smiled and climbed into the driver's seat of my car. As I trailed Chris's vehicle onto the highway, I couldn't stop smiling. I couldn't have been more content with my life, and I was so thankful for Chris's love.

EIGHTEEN

"IS IT A CRIME?"

I sat on the couch next to Carla and watched as Chris and a couple of his bandmates carried boxes out of our apartment.

Chris paused next to the couch on his way out the door. "Dang, baby. How'd you manage to accumulate this much stuff in so little time? You were only living here a few months. This is the *sixth* box."

I rolled my eyes. "Some of that stuff is from my house back in Arkansas and you know it. And besides, you're a big, strong man. That's what those muscles are for. You can handle it." I patted his arm.

He gave me a sly look as he walked toward the door. "I can handle more than that."

"Really now?" I said.

"*Really*, but I can show you better than I can tell you. I mean, this *is* the 'show me state,'" he said as he closed the door behind him.

Carla nudged me. "Oooo, you're gonna get it!"

I shook my head. "He's a mess, really. He talks more game than an NBA announcer."

"Uh-huh, and he sounds like he can back it up, too."

I smiled. "Oh, yeah, I think he can."

"So, y'all are actually gonna do it? You're gonna get married, *for real*?"

I nodded. "Yep, we are."

"Well, I'm excited for you, Marli. I really am, but it just seems so sudden. I mean, y'all have only been dating for a couple of months. You sure you're not rushing things?"

"Carla, I *love* that man. And he loves me. No one has ever made me feel so loved, so special. I didn't even know love like this really existed before him. For the first time in my life, I'm doing something I *know* is right. Chris and I belong together."

"Well, good for you, girl."

"Thanks, Carla. So… have you decided what you're gonna do yet?"

Carla sighed. "I'm gonna finish these three months, and then I'm going home to my boys. No matter how things end up with me and Bryan, I need to be with my kids. I don't know what was wrong with me before, but I really miss them now. I miss being a mother."

I smiled. "You just had a little selfish spell, that's all. It happens to the best of us. I'm just glad you came around, and I really hope you and Bryan can find a way to work it out. You know, my marriage sucked toward the end, but I have to admit that for a while there, I was really happy. It was nice having someone to share my life with. I'm looking forward to having that with Chris."

"Chris really seems like a good man. I pray you two will make it."

"Oh, we will. I really believe this is the man God made just for me."

~*~

Chris sat on the sofa in his living room, staring at me as I placed the photos of Tiffany on the bookshelf.

"What are you looking at?" I asked without turning around to face him.

"The Bible says, 'Whoso findeth a wife findeth a good thing.' I was just looking at my good thing."

I grinned. "I'm not your wife yet."

"One more day." He patted the sofa seat beside him. "Come sit down."

I placed the last photo on the shelf and then joined him on the sofa. "Yes?"

He reached for my hand. "I missed you."

"Chris, I was just across the room."

"But you weren't next to me. I like having you near."

"Well, I'm here now."

He kissed me softly on the lips. "Mm-hmm. You want something to drink? You hungry?"

"I'm okay and if I want something, I can get it myself. This is my home, too, now. Right?"

"It is. I just want you to be comfortable."

"I *am* comfortable. But you're gonna have to do something about *this*." I pointed to the papers scattered about the granite-topped coffee table.

"Aw, that? It's just some bills and stuff."

"*That's* a mess. Can I at least stack it up neatly?"

He leaned over and kissed me again. "You can do whatever you want to do. Like you said, this is your home now." He stood from the couch. "I'ma get me something to drink. You sure you don't want something?"

I shook my head. "I'm fine."

"Okay, be right back."

I smiled and watched him leave the room then started stacking the papers on the table. It was mostly bills and store receipts, but then I came across the bill of sale for his Navigator. *Ticket price $55,000.* I shook my head. *That's ridiculous for a car*, I thought. I read further down and noticed that it said, *Financed amount: $0. Balance paid in full*. He paid for the car outright? No financing? I laid the paper on the table and stood up. How could he have paid cash for that truck? Where did he get the money?

I was still standing next to the sofa when Chris returned to the living room holding two drinks in his hand.

He sat down. "I brought you something anyway."

I looked down at him but didn't say a word.

"Baby, you all right? You look like you just saw a ghost," he said.

"I... I just saw something that I don't understand."

He stood up and placed his hands on my arms. "What is it? What's wrong?"

"The bill of sale for the Navigator. You paid cash for it? Fifty-five thousand dollars cash? How could you afford to do that?"

Chris reached down and picked up the paper. He looked at me and shook his head. "It's not what you think."

I backed away from him. "Don't tell me you *saved* fifty-five thousand dollars or that you *saved* the money for this ring or this apartment. Where did you get the money, Chris? I can't marry you if you're gonna keep lying to me."

"Okay, okay, listen. I haven't been totally honest with you about some things. The truth is that I really don't make that much money with the band."

"Then what are you doing, Chris?" I asked, my voice raising an octave.

"I'm not doing what you think. I'm not selling drugs."

"Then what are you doing?!"

"Sit down."

"No. I'll stand."

"Come on, Marli. Just sit down, baby," he pleaded.

I sighed. "Chris, just tell me."

"I will. Come sit down, *please*."

I hesitantly slumped onto the couch and folded my arms.

"Okay, so um, when my parents died they left me some money."

"*Some* money?"

He dropped his head. "Well, a lotta money, actually."

I frowned. "Really? How much, Chris?"

"Um, enough that we should never have to work or want for anything for the rest of our lives."

"How much are we talking here, Chris? Three hundred thousand? Four hundred thousand? A million? Because that won't last the rest of your life in this economy. Especially the way you're spending it."

He shifted on the couch and cleared his throat. "No, those would be gross underestimates." He picked up a pen and an envelope from the table. He jotted down a figure and handed the envelope to me. "More like that much."

I was glad I sat down.

"What?! What in the hell did your folks do for a living? Rob banks?"

He shrugged. "It's old money. My real father's family owned a bunch of oil wells in Texas and the Gulf. You ever heard of Russell Oil and Fuel? Well, I'm Russell. I'm the only surviving heir, so it all belongs to me. Plus, I took some of the money and invested it—bought some businesses."

"Businesses?" I felt dizzy. I just couldn't believe my ears. I was happy and sad at the same time—happy because, well, he was rich. Sad because he'd kept it from me.

He shrugged again. "Um... yeah, I own a couple of Taco Bells, um, a McDonald's, a Mercedes dealership, and—"

"Chris?! Why didn't you tell me?! Better yet, were you *ever* gonna tell me?"

"Yeah, I was gonna tell you… eventually."

"What were you gonna do? Hand me a prenup to sign during the ceremony? Don't you think this is something I needed to know?"

Chris sighed. "Well, yeah, but in the past when I told people, they'd start acting all different. I stopped telling people long ago. I never even told Russell's mother. I just didn't think that it really mattered."

"Chris, if you didn't trust me enough to tell me this, why would you want to marry me?"

Chris sat up and shook his head. "No, baby. I trust you. I… I don't know what I was thinking. I guess I was afraid it would change your perception of me."

"To what? *I love you*, Chris, no matter what your bank account says, and I certainly wasn't gonna be mad at you for having money. I'm just not sure now if *you* really love *me*."

Chris leaned forward. "Wait… wait, don't say that. I love you. I love you with all my heart. You *know* that."

I shook my head. "No, I *don't* know, Chris. Maybe we're rushing things. Maybe I shouldn't have moved in here. I mean, how well do we really know each other? I… I don't want another failed marriage."

Chris grabbed my hand. "I know you're sweet and caring and beautiful and sexy. I know you like cupcakes, and you like to sing along with the radio. You like to hold hands, and your smile brightens my day. I know I love you. I know that without a doubt. And I know that you love me. We *won't* fail."

I shook my head.

"Okay," he said, "Ask me anything. What do you want to know?"

"All right, when were you gonna tell me about the money?"

"I don't know. Before we got married?"

"What about a prenup?"

He frowned. "I don't want one."

"Come on, Chris. You can't be serious. You're gonna marry me without protecting your money when you didn't even trust me enough to tell me about it?"

"Stop saying that! I *do* trust you, and I'm not concerned about that money. My parents taught me long ago what's important in life, and money ain't it. Marli, we're getting married, not closing some business deal. I'm not gonna ask you to sign some contract or agreement. I've prayed about this and I trust that God will keep us together. Divorce is not even an option as far as I'm concerned. I'm getting married to *stay* married. *I love you*, baby. Can't you see that?"

"Chris, I want to believe you, but—"

"No buts, just believe me. Believe in *us*."

"Believe in us? How? If you can keep something like this from me, what's to stop you from keeping something else from me? How do I know you don't have another woman or something?"

His eyes widened. "Another woman? What the hell? Where did that even come from?"

"It came from the fact that you like to keep secrets from me."

"Secrets? No, secret—*singular*. I kept *one* thing from you, and I'm sorry. You just went to another level with this other woman stuff."

I stood to my feet. "That *one* thing you kept from me had a whole lotta zeros hanging off the end of it!"

Chris stood to face me. "And I said *I'm sorry*! But how did we get from that to me cheating. That's just crazy!" he said, raising his voice at me.

I rolled my eyes. "Crazy, huh?"

"Yes, *crazy*. I understand you're upset, but you know better than that. You *know* I don't have anyone else."

"What's *crazy* is that I have no idea what you're doing when you travel with the band. You gonna stand here and tell me that women don't approach you, Chris?"

"I didn't say that. Of course they do. Women approach me all the time. But it doesn't matter. I got what I want and that's *you*, baby!"

"So you say."

He threw up his hands. "Come on! Are you serious right now? You wanna know what I do when I'm on the road? I play my damn horn, eat, sleep, and talk to you on the phone. *That's it*! You *know* that. I ain't got no other woman, Marli."

"Whether you have another woman or not, you *lied* to me, Chris. *You lied to me.* I *told* you I can't stand to be lied to."

He rubbed the back of his neck. "Well, technically, it wasn't a lie. I just withheld a fact. I never said I was broke, Marli. I said I had some money saved up, I just never said how much."

"No, technically, you *lied*."

I was mad and hurt. I felt betrayed and played and I needed to get out of there. So I walked over to the door, snatched it open, and left his condo. I'd made it halfway down the hall to the elevator when I realized I had no shoes on my feet, no car keys in my hand, and no idea where I was going. I stopped, leaned against the wall, and closed my eyes.

A second later, I heard Chris's voice. "Come back, baby. I'm sorry if I upset you. I'm sorry for raising my voice at you. I love you. Just... just come back."

I opened my eyes, saw the sadness in his, and sighed. "Chris, what are we doing? We're moving way too fast. We don't know each other well enough. This is all just *too fast*."

He leaned against the wall next to me. "Okay," he said, "We can slow things down. We can wait and get married later. Whatever you wanna do. Let's just get to know each other better for right now. I... I just don't wanna lose you." He reached for my hand. "Come back, baby."

I loved him, and I wanted to be with him. What was I supposed to do? I took his hand and followed him back into his condo. Once inside, I sat on the couch and buried my face in my hands. "Look, we can slow things down like you said, but I don't wanna be shacking up here in the meantime. I should've never moved in here like this. I'll just go back to my apartment."

He shook his head. "No, I'll go. I'll get a room or something if you want me to. I said this is your home, and I meant it. Stay here. I'll go."

I sighed. "No, this is *your* home. I'll just sleep on the sofa until we can figure this out."

Chris leaned over and kissed my cheek. "I'm sorry for not telling you about the money and for lying to you, but I'm glad you know now."

I nodded and then leaned back on the sofa and closed my eyes, signaling that I was done talking. I'd had enough conversation for one night.

Of course Chris wouldn't let me sleep on the couch, just as I knew he wouldn't. I slept in the bedroom, and he took the couch. I found it hard to sleep that night. I couldn't help but wonder what a future with Chris would actually mean. For the first time in a long time, I started to have some serious doubts about our relationship.

NINETEEN

"IT'S ONLY LOVE THAT GETS YOU THROUGH"

A couple of weeks later, I finally mustered up the nerve to call Carla and tell her about what was going on with Chris. I'd been hesitant to tell her, afraid to hear her say, "I told you so." Afraid to have to confirm that she was right—we *were* moving too fast.

I gave her the basic facts—he was rich and he didn't tell me. Carla's only response was, "Wow." Then she asked if we could meet up during one of our breaks at work to talk. She wanted to hear everything—in detail. Of course I agreed. I needed to talk about things so that I could figure out what to *do* about things. We met in the cafeteria that evening and, over turkey sandwiches and weak hospital coffee, I gave her a full account of what had happened—from my discovery of the bill of sale for his truck, to the news that he was a doggone oil mogul.

"You were right. We've really been rushing things, Carla," I said.

Carla nodded and shifted in her seat. After taking a sip of her coffee she said, "I knew you'd get around to it eventually."

I frowned a little. "Get around to what?"

She sighed. "You finally figured out a way to mess things up with him. He's so good; you had to twist some stuff around just to make him seem bad. But you did it."

I straightened my posture. "What? Are you crazy?"

"Not now. Not today. Today, I'm *very* sane."

"Then what are you talking about? He *lied*, Carla. He lied about something *really important*."

"He didn't lie. He omitted a fact."

I leaned forward. "No, he lied by omission. You don't do that unless you have something to hide. He hid the fact that he had money from me. No telling what else he's hiding."

"You don't think you deserve him. That's why you're doing this."

"What?!" Was she out of her mind?

"You think he's too good for you. That's what it's always been about with you. That's why you settled for noncommittal booty calls instead of real relationships. That's why you slept with every Tom, Dick, and Darius in the tri-state area. You have let what Tim did to you and all of the horrible things your parents said to you convince you that you do not deserve happiness or love. You really believe that you don't deserve this tall, handsome, *rich* man. So instead of putting a freakin' full page ad in the newspaper back home announcing that you hit the jackpot in every possible way with this man, what do you do? Your crazy ass pushes him away. I bet you even went so far as to accuse him of cheating."

I slammed my hand down on the table, bringing attention to us, but I didn't care. "Carla! Who do you—"

"Who do I think I am? *I'm* your best friend, the friend who's known you since elementary school. *I'm* the one who knows you better than anyone else in the world. I know you better than you know yourself! Yeah, I know I'm crazy. Hell, at least I can admit it. But you? You actually think what you're doing makes sense. So he didn't tell you he was rich? So-the hell-what? Can you blame him? Do you have any idea what it must be like to have that kind of money? Can you imagine what would happen if every woman he dated knew?"

"We're not dating. We're *engaged*," I said through my teeth.

"And you're sitting over there with the Rock of Gibraltar on your doggone finger. You should be on your knees right now thanking Jesus and God and all of the angels in Heaven that this man pursued you and wooed you and showed you what real love is, because we both know that wham-bam-thank-you-ma'am-dang-you-pregnant-so-I-guess-we'll-get-married relationship you had with Tim was *not* love."

I closed my eyes, tried to calm myself. "Carla—"

"As a matter of fact, you should be doing a holy dance right now. And then, after that, you need to pass out in the spirit. And after that, you need to run—not walk—to the altar with him."

"You were the one who asked if we were rushing things!"

"I was wrong that day, but not today."

"Carla," I said calmly, "We were *literally* a day away from getting married and he still hadn't told me about his money."

She rolled her eyes. "But he *did* tell you."

"Only after I pressed the issue."

"And he doesn't even want a prenup! He's a *good man*, Marli! Come on! What is it? Does he just like thick girls? Shoot, let me gain some weight and take him off your hands. I'll show you *exactly* how to handle this situation."

My eyes narrowed. "Carla, you done crossed the damn line, now. You're talking about the man I love."

Carla stood from the table. "Then act like it."

And with that, she flounced out of the cafeteria.

For the rest of my shift, I was troubled by Carla's words. She'd been harsh and blunt with me. But as the night wore on, I came to realize there was some validity to what Carla had said. Maybe I *was* sabotaging this relationship on purpose. But what was I going to do to fix it?

~*~

The next morning after I made it home from work, I couldn't sleep. So while Chris left for his daily workout, I cooked him a big, country breakfast and as soon as I heard the front door close signaling his return home, I called for him.

"Yeah, baby?" he answered as he walked into the kitchen. When he saw the spread I'd prepared for him, his face lit up.

"This looks good, baby. You did all this for me?"

I walked over to him and wrapped my arms around him as I reached up and planted a soft kiss on his lips. "Yes. Just for you."

He smiled down at me. "Well, what did I do to deserve this?"

"Nothing. It's my way of apologizing. I'm sorry. I… I guess I overreacted about the whole money thing. I just… I just wish you'd told me sooner."

He nodded. "I know. I really am sorry about that. I'll never do anything like that again."

I smiled up at him. "Good. Come on so we can eat. I have something else to tell you."

He took a seat at the table, reached for a plate, and looked up at me. "Well, one thing's for sure, I know you're not gonna tell me you're pregnant."

I laughed. "*No,* I wanna get married tomorrow."

He sprung up from the table and hugged me tightly.

"Are you for real, baby?" he asked.

I closed my eyes and squeezed him tightly. "Yeah, I am. I love you, and I'm more than ready to marry you. I traded with someone, so I'm going in to work again tonight. I'll be off tomorrow night, instead, for the honeymoon."

He grinned. "Oh, yeah, *the honeymoon*. Thank you, baby. You just made my day—hell, you just made my *life*! I'ma go call my folks right now."

"Okay," I said and watched him jog into the living room.

He returned a few minutes later with instructions from his mother to report to his parents' house immediately after we left the courthouse. His father would marry us after we got the marriage license. We spent the rest of the day talking and planning. Honeymoon in New York—Broadway and shopping, and maybe a European cruise after that. It was, hands down, one of the happiest days of my life.

~*~

"How's work?" Chris asked.

"Busy as ever. I miss you. Can't wait to be Mrs. Christopher King," I said.

"Miss you, too, baby, and I can't wait to be your husband. You know what else?"

"No, what?"

"I can't wait to get you in that honeymoon suite. My daddy says that sex is a gift for marriage. I *can't wait* to unwrap my present tomorrow. Girl, I'ma put it on you!"

I giggled. "You better not be playing."

"Baby, when I get done with you, you ain't never gonna want to leave my bed again. I promise you that."

I lowered my voice as a coworker passed by. "I could say the same thing, Chris. I got a few tricks up my sleeve, you know."

"Damn, really, baby?"

"*Really.*"

"Well, let me go run some laps or lift some weights or something so I'll be prepared."

"You might wanna drink a protein shake, too."

"Girl, you keep talking like that and I'ma bring my dad up there and marry you tonight! You know how long I've been dreaming about this? How much longer is your shift?"

"Six hours."

"I'm counting down."

"Me, too. Let me get off of this phone and get back to work. I love you."

"Love you, too. Call me if you get another break."

"Okay."

I was smiling as I hung up the phone. I sat there in the break room for a few minutes and thought about how blessed I was to have Chris in my life. I was so thankful and so happy that I almost couldn't believe it. It almost seemed unreal to be that much in love.

I didn't get to bask in my happiness for long, though. As soon as I stepped foot back into the ER, I was called into one of the trauma rooms to assist with a child who'd been brought in by his mother.

The child was in respiratory arrest. I especially hated to see children in distress, but as usual, I sucked it up and hurriedly walked into the trauma room. I approached the gurney to relieve one of the other nurses, Pam. "What's his status?" I asked.

"Eight-year-old asthmatic. Evidently, he had an asthma attack and the mother took some time trying out different inhalers only to find them all empty. By the time she got him here, he was in full respiratory arrest," said Pam.

I looked down at the little boy and shook my head. "Poor kid."

Pam nodded. "Yeah. Dr. Price is *livid*. You know how he is about kids. I'm sure he's gonna call child services once we get him stabilized."

"He should."

I pushed air into his lungs with the Ambu bag and said a silent prayer for him. He was pale, brown-skinned with a mass of curly, black hair on his head. His keen nose and thin lips told me that he was probably of mixed race. As I studied him, I noticed something oddly familiar about him. He reminded me of someone…

"Hold on!" Dr. Price shouted. "Stop bagging him. He's coughing."

I'd been so engrossed in my own thoughts about the boy that I hadn't noticed him coughing. I stopped bagging him and sure enough, he was breathing on his own. They were ragged breaths, but they were breaths nonetheless. I smiled and let out the breath I didn't even realized I was holding. Dr. Price leaned over the boy and opened his eyes to check his pupils. It was then that I realized why the child seemed so familiar to me. His eyes were a beautiful shade of blue.

Dr. Price announced that the child's pupils were equal and reactive and then ordered for someone to get him an ICU bed. I looked over at Pam who held the child's chart.

"What's his name?" I asked softly.

Pam gave me a confused look. "Who? The kid?"

"Yeah, *what's his name?*"

"Okay, calm down. Let's see." She flipped through the chart.

"Uh, Russell C. King."

"Okay, um, I'll be right back." I popped the gloves off of my hands and headed toward the nurses' station.

Behind me, Pam yelled something about calling upstairs for a bed for the boy. I was headed to the phone, but I knew the ICU wouldn't be the first place I called. I picked up the receiver, but before I could dial Chris's number, a woman approached the desk with a frantic look on her face.

"Ma'am, you were in there with my baby. Is he all right?"

I looked up at her and laid the phone down. "Um, he's stable. I'm getting ready to call for him a bed. He's gonna have to go to ICU."

"ICU? I thought you said he was stable. Can't I take him home now?"

"Well, Dr. Price wants to keep him. He really needs to be monitored closely, and he can't go home without an inhaler."

She nodded. "Yeah, yeah I know. I left it back home. We're just here in town visiting. I need to talk to the doctor."

I looked down at the phone and then back up at her face. She was short and heavy-set, which seemed to be Chris's preference. Her skin was a little lighter than mine. She looked like she'd once been pretty, but something in her life had beaten her down and taken away from her looks. Her round eyes had bags underneath them, and her full lips were dry.

"Um, let me go and get him," I said. I hurried back into the trauma room to get Dr. Price. I returned to the desk to find her standing in the same spot, nervously tapping her foot.

"Um, Dr. Price will be right out to talk to you, Ms.—" I stopped on purpose, hoping she'd fill in the blank.

"Thank you," she said, without giving me her name.

Dr. Price, however, was able to get it from her. "Ms. King?" he said as he approached her.

"No, it's Franklin," she replied.

I tuned the rest of their conversation out, turned my back to them, quickly called up to ICU to get the bed assignment, and then I dialed Chris's number.

As soon as the call connected, he said, "Hey, baby. Break time, again, already?"

"Chris," I whispered, "You need to get down here *right now*."

"What is it? Why are you whispering? What's going on?"

"Listen, I think Russell is here in the ER."

"My *son*, Russell?" he asked, sounding shocked.

"Yeah, get off the phone and come *now*. His mom is trying to leave with him."

"I'm coming."

Click.

When I turned around, both Dr. Price and Fatima were gone. I got up from my seat and walked to Russell's room only to find the stretcher empty.

"Where's the kid who was just here?" I asked Pam.

"You mean the King kid? His mom just stormed in here and took him home, AMA."

"What?! When?!"

"A few seconds ago. Dr. Price called security, but she made it out the employee exit before they could get here."

"Dang-it!"

"Marli, you all right? You're getting a little too involved with this kid, aren't you?"

I was only half listening to her. "Yeah, I guess. Look, I need to take my break. Be right back."

Before Pam could reply, I walked out to the parking lot to see if I could spot Fatima and Russell anywhere. I was still out there when Chris pulled up to the front of the ER.

I trotted over to his car. "Chris!"

He turned around with a wide-eyed expression on his face. "What're you doing out here? How's Russ?" he asked.

"He's gone. She took him."

"What?! Are you sure it was him? How could you have recognized him?"

"He was admitted under his real name and he looks just like you. He has the same blue eyes. His mother said her last name was Franklin. Was that Fatima's name?"

"Yeah, Fatima Franklin. How long they been gone?"

"Not long. She snuck out with him just in the time I was on the phone with you."

Chris slumped against his car and placed his head in his hands. "Damn! I got here as quick as I could." He looked up at me. "How long were they here?"

I placed my hand over his. "He wasn't breathing when he got here, and it took a few minutes to get him stabilized. After I left his room, I talked to his mom and called up to get a bed for him. The next call I made was to you."

He moved his hands and looked at me. "Why did you wait to call me? You should've called me the second you recognized him!"

I backed up a little. "Well, at first I wasn't sure it *was* him. When I was sure, I called you."

"Sure or not, if you even *thought* it was Russell you should've called me. This is the closest I've been to seeing him in five years!

Damn, Marli."

I frowned. "Are you mad at me or something? I did the best I could in the situation. I wasn't even supposed to call you. I could get in trouble for it. It's against the privacy policy."

He gave me a look I'd never seen on his face before. "You were worried about this *job*? I told you that you could quit this job. My son is more important than any job. He's more important than—" He shook his head. "I don't have time for this. Did you at least call the police?"

"Well, no. It all happened so fast…"

"Look, I gotta go. I need to call the police and tell them what happened."

"Okay, Chris, I'm sorry. I didn't know what else to do."

Without a word, he climbed back into his car and left. I stood there for a moment and tried to process what had just happened. Then I walked over to one of the benches outside and prayed for Chris. I knew that much of what he'd said was due to the pain he was in. I told myself not to internalize it, but it'd hurt my feelings for him to attack me like that.

I sat there for ten minutes, praying for the man I loved and his son, before returning to the ER.

TWENTY

"THE MOON AND THE SKY"

By the time my shift ended the next morning, I really wasn't sure if Chris was going to pick me up. He hadn't called even once since leaving the ER, and he hadn't answered any of my calls. Sure enough, when I walked out the lobby doors, there was no sign of him. I stood and looked around for a moment and then sat on a bench and dialed his number—no answer. I sighed and rested my back against the seat. *I should've driven my car.* I sat for twenty minutes before finally deciding to call Carla. Luckily, I caught her before she left the hospital. During the ride home, I filled her in on what had happened with Russell.

"Man, Marli, I bet Chris is really upset," she said.

"Yeah, but he seems more upset with me than anything. If I didn't know any better, I'd think he blamed me for the whole thing."

She shook her head. "No, he doesn't. He's just upset and worried about his son. Everything'll be okay. You just be there for him."

I nodded. "Of course I will."

A few minutes later, I stepped out of Carla's vehicle and made my way up to the fifth floor. I let myself into the condo and dropped my purse by the front door.

"Chris!" I yelled. "Chris, I'm home!"

"In here!"

I breathed a sigh of relief. When I couldn't hear from him, I'd started to worry. I walked into the bedroom to find him busily packing a suitcase.

"Are you going somewhere?" I asked.

"Yeah, the police think Fatima's been living in Chicago. Right under my damn nose!" He paused and shook his head. "Anyway, a boy fitting Russ's description was admitted to a hospital there early this morning. I booked a flight. I'm leaving in a few minutes," he said.

"Well, I'll go with you. Give me a second to throw some things in a bag."

He looked up at me for a second and then resumed packing his bag. "Naw, you stay. No sense in uprooting both of us. It may not even be him."

"I don't care, Chris. I wanna be there for you."

He zipped up the bag and lifted it off of the bed. "I don't want you to go."

I frowned. "What? Why?"

"Look, Marli. I need to do this alone. He's not your son *or* your concern."

"He *is* my concern. He's your son so that *makes* him my concern. Why are you acting like this?"

He released an exasperated sigh. "Like *what*, Marli?"

"Like you're mad at me. Are you upset with me about something?"

He shook his head. "No. I just know I can't expect you to be too concerned about Russ. Your child's already all grown up. Why would you wanna worry yourself with my kid?"

"Chris, what are you talking about? You know I'm not like that. Why are you saying this stuff?"

Chris sighed. "Look, I don't have time to go round and round about this with you. I need to go and try to get my son back. I need to focus on this instead of other things."

"Other things being me? So I've just been a distraction? Is that what you're getting at, Chris?"

He walked over to me and peered down at my face. "Like I said, I don't have time for this right now."

I followed him from the bedroom out into the hallway. "When will you be back?"

"When I find my son."

"And what should I do?"

He turned and looked me in the eye. "Whatever you want. I really don't care," he said, slamming the door behind him.

I walked over to the couch and sat down, tears rolling down my cheeks. The look in Chris's eyes had been so cold and detached. Maybe it *was* my fault he'd missed seeing his son. Maybe I should've called him as soon as I recognized him. Or maybe I should've called the police. Maybe I really *had* distracted him from finding Russ.

I sat there for over an hour, deep in thought and despair, before my exhaustion finally overtook me.

~*~

I sat up on the sofa, feeling a little disoriented. After a few seconds, it registered in my mind that my phone was ringing and I picked it up from the coffee table. I didn't recognize the number.

"Hello?" I said through a yawn.

"Marli?" said a female voice on the other end.

"Yes. Who's this?"

"It's Ava. Chris's sister."

I leaned forward. "Ava? What's going on?"

"It's Russell."

"Chris found him?" *Oh dear Lord, please let him have found him.*

"Yes, he found him in Chicago."

"Oh, *thank God.*"

"Marli, Russell... he didn't make it."

"What?" I doubled over on the sofa. It felt like someone had punched me in the gut.

"Fatima drove Russ all the way to Chicago without an inhaler. He had another asthma attack, and by the time she got him to the hospital, it was too late for them to save him. He's... he's gone. He was already gone when Chris got there."

I placed my hand over my mouth. "*Oh, no.* Oh, Lord no! Where's Chris? Is he okay?"

"He's in pretty bad shape. My dad went to get him," Ava said, her voice breaking.

I felt my eyes begin to fill with tears. "Okay. I'll be here when he gets home."

"I'm glad. He needs you. Bye, Marli."

"Bye."

I spent the next few hours pacing around the condo, or sitting on the couch and crying, or cleaning up the already spotless rooms. By the time Chris finally made it home, I was very close to losing my mind. When I heard him walk through the door, I raced from the kitchen to meet him. He looked at me with weary, exhausted eyes and dropped his bags by the door.

I reached up and wrapped my arms around his neck as he collapsed against me. I rubbed the back of his head as he buried his face in my chest and dissolved into tears. He let out a loud, painful, heart-wrenching wail.

"Oh, baby. I don't know what to do!" he groaned. His body shook as he clawed at my shirt as if trying to find something, *anything* to grasp onto.

I squeezed him tightly, tried to sooth him with my voice. "I'm here. I'm here for you. I'm not going anywhere."

"Oh, God! *Oh, God!* Help me... *please*, help me! Please, *please*, help me!" he pleaded over and over again. *"Please...* somebody help me!"

Help him, God. Please help him, I prayed.

He gripped me tightly, as if letting me go would be the death of him. He yelled and screamed and moaned until he was hoarse. And then we slid to the floor, and I spent the night holding him and crying with him.

TWENTY-ONE

"HANG ON TO YOUR LOVE"

"Where is he now?" Carla asked. She'd finished her assignment and was back in Arkansas with her boys. She and Bryan were trying to work things out but were still separated.

I pulled the phone from my ear and stepped into the kitchen doorway. From there I could see Chris sitting in his usual spot on the sofa.

I reclaimed my seat at the kitchen table. "He's on the couch. He just sits there all day long, watching TV until bedtime."

"So he's not any better? It's been, what, two months now?"

I sighed. "Yeah. He's just having a hard time coping. He blames himself for not trying harder to find Russell. He thinks if he'd found him earlier, he'd still be alive."

"He doesn't really believe that, does he? He's got to know that it's not his fault."

"A lot of what Chris knows is in the back of his mind. He's just blocking it out. He's... he's just not Chris anymore. I don't know *who* he is."

"I'm sorry, Marli."

I placed my elbow on the table and my free hand on my forehead. "And the worst thing is that I don't know how to get him back. He hasn't picked up a Bible since Russell died, won't step foot in a church. He's cancelled all of the band's shows. He just sits and stares at the TV or stares into space. He won't talk to me. The only thing he *will* do with me is have sex with me."

"Whoa, wait a minute. I thought you two were waiting until after you got married or did I miss something? Did you get married and forget to tell me?"

"No. After all that's happened, I just don't think it would be right to bring up us getting married. It just seems selfish."

"Well, who brought up y'all having sex?"

"Um, I did. I just wanted to help him, Carla. I would've done anything to make him feel better. So one night it just happened. Now it happens all the time, several times a day."

"Several times a day? Dang, girl. You must've really put it on him."

"Carla…"

"Seriously, Marli, I don't know how you held out so long in the first place. You have the discipline of a nun."

"*Carla...*"

"Okay, okay, just tell me this, is he any good?"

"*Very.*"

"*Daaaang*, girl."

"Carla!"

"Okay, sorry. Look, if you feel so bad about it, don't do it."

"To be honest, it's the only connection I have with him now. Like I said, he won't talk to me or even look at me otherwise. I never dreamed things would end up like this. I was supposed to be his wife but now I feel more like a jump-off."

"No, you're definitely not a jump-off. Jump-off's don't get marriage proposals or big rings, and they don't get to live in luxury condos."

I sighed. "What am I gonna do, Carla? I just want my old Chris back. That's all I want."

"Stop trying to make him better. Stop trying to fix him."

"And do what, Carla? Sit back and watch him disappear? Desert him? I love him. I can't do that."

"I didn't say desert him. But what you're doing now is enabling him to stay in that rut. Pray for him, be there for him. Doing things that you know are wrong just to try to make him happy won't help him."

I shut my eyes tightly and rubbed my forehead. "Yeah, you're right. Look, I need to get off and see if he'll eat some dinner. Pray for us. I'll talk to you later."

"Sure thing. Bye, girl."

"Bye."

I walked into the living room and stood next to the couch. "You hungry, Chris? I made lasagna."

Chris looked up at me and shook his head. "No, I'm not hungry."

"Okay, well, there's plenty. Let me know if you get hungry. You need to eat, baby."

I turned to leave, but before I could, he grabbed my arm.

"Come sit down with me," he said as he looked up at me. His eyes were still so full of sadness.

I smiled down at him. "Okay."

I sat down, and Chris grasped my hand. I looked into his eyes as he brought my hand to his lips and kissed it.

"I love you, Chris," I whispered.

His lips moved from my hand to my arm. "I love you, too," he murmured. I closed my eyes as he worked his way up my arm to my neck then my lips. "I love every single inch of you, Marli."

I looked up at him as he stood and began to undress. I knew I'd feel guilty afterward, but at that moment, I wanted nothing more than to be with Chris in that way—to hold him, to touch him, and to love him.

"I want to help you feel better," I said.

He sat back down next to me and kissed me. "You *do* make me feel better."

"I do?"

"Yes. You do." He looked me in the eye as he undressed me. "*This* makes me feel better." He pulled me into a tight embrace, his warm skin soothing mine. "I love you so much, baby. Don't ever leave me."

"I won't."

"Good, because I won't ever let you go."

"Neither will I."

I closed my eyes as we slid from the couch to the floor… and Chris and I comforted each other the only way we knew how.

TWENTY-TWO

"TURN MY BACK ON YOU"

After another month or so of a sorrowful existence with Chris, I was thankful that Tiffany was coming to St. Louis for a visit. I hoped her presence would help to lift the dark cloud that loomed over our lives. But even in that hope, the heaviness of my heart remained.

On my way to the airport to pick her up that day, I decided to make a quick stop. I stepped into the sanctuary of Rev. King's church, sat near the back, and prayed. It was Wednesday afternoon, and the sanctuary was open to the public.

I sat there and fought back tears. I was worn and tired and I felt so alone. I loved Chris more than I could explain. I wanted so badly for us to return to what we'd once had. But he just seemed so distant, and the pressure of trying to carry him had begun to make me physically ill. I was having trouble keeping food down, and I'd started to lose weight.

I leaned forward and rested my forehead on the back of the pew in front of me and closed my eyes. I prayed and prayed until I felt a hand on my shoulder. I looked up to see Rev. King standing next to me.

I wiped my eyes and stood to my feet. "Oh, hi, Rev. King. I... I was just leaving."

I felt embarrassed about being seen in such a mess and, besides, I was pretty sure he and his wife didn't think too well of me since Chris and I had been living together for months. Most Sundays, after church, I made it a point to avoid them, which was a stark contrast to the many Sunday dinners I'd once shared with them.

He placed his hand on my arm. "Wait, can I speak with you for a moment, Marli?"

I sat back down on the pew.

"How's Chris doing? He won't return any of my calls," he said with a concerned look on his face.

Before I could answer, I dissolved into tears. Rev. King put his arm around my shoulders to comfort me. When my tears had finally ceased, he moved his arm and looked me in the eye.

"Marli, has Chris talked to you at all about what happened?"

I shook my head. "No, sir—not really. We don't do much talking anymore."

He nodded. "How are *you* feeling?"

I released a ragged sigh. "Tired and helpless. I want so badly to help Chris. I just don't know what to do."

"Were you praying for him just now?"

"Yes, sir. I was praying for *both* of us."

"Then that's the best thing you can do for him—for both of you. We've all been praying for him. Chris is stronger than he seems. He's had to deal with death almost ever since he's been in this world. I know he'll work through this. Stay by his side and support him. He's blessed to have you in his life. He'll come around."

I exhaled deeply. "I hope you're right. I miss him *so much*."

He smiled at me. "So do I. Where are you headed after this? You should come over to the house for dinner."

"Um, I'm gonna pick my daughter up from the airport in a little bit."

"Great. Bring her along. We'd love to meet her."

I offered him a weak smile. "Okay, I will."

~*~

I sat outside the airport in Chris's Navigator and waited for Tiffany's flight to arrive. Though Christmas was only days away, it felt like it was years away. I thought about what Carla and Rev. King had said, but I was honestly beginning to think that I was spinning my wheels. I wondered if maybe I wasn't what Chris needed. Maybe my presence was only making things worse for him. Maybe I should've left long ago.

I was staring out the windshield and had just decided to walk into the airport when my phone rang. It was my father. I hadn't talked to him since the day he met Chris. I hadn't wanted to talk to him, either. I stared at the phone for a moment and then pressed the button to answer the call. I held it to my ear but didn't speak.

"Hello? Marli?" my father said.

"Yes."

"Oh, I wasn't sure if you answered or if the call had disconnected."

I didn't reply.

My father cleared his throat. "Um, how've you been?"

"Fine."

"Well, that's good. And Chris?"

I was surprised he even remembered Chris's name. "He's okay."

"Really? I talk to Tiff just about every week. She told me that he lost his son. I'm very sorry to hear that."

"Um… well, thank you." He was being surprisingly kind and

normal. What was his deal?

"Well, I hate to hear of anyone losing a child. I don't know what I'd do if something happened to you or Justine."

I paused for a second, still surprised by his words. "Well, Chris is all right, considering."

"Good. He's a good man."

Things had finally reached the top of the weirded-out scale. "Um, Dad? What's going on?"

"What do you mean?"

"The way you're talking? Saying all those nice things? What's the deal?"

"Marli, you're my daughter and I haven't heard from you in months. When Tiffany told me what happened, I was concerned."

"Well, thanks for calling. We're all right."

"Well, stick with him. He's a good man, and he obviously loves you. He certainly didn't back down to me, and I can respect that."

"*Really?*" I scoffed. "It would've been nice if you would've let Chris know you approved of him."

"Hopefully, I'll be able to tell him one day."

I hesitated, and then said, "And it would've been nice if you hadn't said all of that horrible stuff about me."

Silence.

I sighed. "Okay... well, I need to get off now. Tiff's plane just landed—"

"Wait... I... um, I apologize for saying those things. I was caught a little off-guard by Chris. He just didn't seem like your type."

"And what exactly *is* my type, Dad?"

"I don't... I don't know."

"Then what you just said doesn't make any sense and it's not the truth." I felt my eyes begin to well up. "You said those things because that's honestly how you feel about me. You think I'm unlovable and unacceptable and... and it hurts. It's *always* hurt for you to say those things to me."

"I didn't know... I'm sorry," he said softly.

"Yeah, well, I just needed to get that off my chest. I need to go now."

"Okay. I love you, Marli. I hope you know that."

I wiped my wet face, released a sigh. "I do. Bye, Dad."

I ended the call and then headed into the airport to meet Tiffany.

~*~

On the way from the airport to Chris's parents' house, I was quiet as Tiffany chattered away about Spelman and all of the friends she'd made.

"Mama, you okay?" she asked.

I glanced at her. "Yeah, I'm all right. I'm glad to see you. I missed you."

She smiled. "I missed you, too. How's Chris?"

I sighed. "He's the same."

"He'll come around. Just give him some time."

I nodded and pulled into Rev. King's driveway. We walked up to the door and were greeted by Chris's mom who hugged both of us tightly before leading us into the house. We walked into the living room where I introduced Tiffany to Rev. King, then we all took a seat while Rev. and Mrs. King asked Tiffany about Spelman. During the conversation, I have to admit that I pretty much just zoned out. I felt like I was in a fog. Chris had been in so much misery, I honestly think it had rubbed off on me.

"Marli?" Mrs. King said.

I snapped out of my haze and looked around the room. Evidently, Mrs. King had called my name more than once. Everyone was staring at me.

"Um, ma'am?" I said.

Rev. King frowned. "Marli, are you okay?"

"Yes, sir. I'm fine," I answered.

He glanced at his wife then back at me. "Lizzie was just saying that dinner should be ready in a few more minutes."

I looked at him for a moment. "Actually, I think I should get back to Chris. He'll be wondering where I am."

"Why don't you let me deal with Chris? He needs to get out of that apartment, himself. I'll call him. You just sit tight." He looked at his phone and then up at me. "Let me call him on your phone, Marli. Maybe he'll answer if he thinks it's you."

I handed him my phone and sat and watched as he dialed Chris's number. From what I heard of Rev. King's side of the conversation, Chris wasn't going anywhere, and he wasn't too happy about me being there, either.

"Well, she can bring you a plate then," Mr. King said. And then, after a long pause: "Chris, she'll be back. It's just dinner." And after another pause, "Okay, I'll tell her."

Rev. King ended the call and handed the phone back to me. "Um, Marli, he's pretty upset about you not being there. And he says he has something he needs to tell you."

I nodded and picked up my purse. "Okay. Come on, Tiff."

Mrs. King stood and said, "Marli, why don't you let Tiffany stay here and have dinner with us? We'll bring her over later. Besides, I'd like to see Chris. He hasn't been over in weeks."

I looked over at Tiffany who nodded in agreement.

"Okay," I said. "I'll see you soon." Then, out of the blue, a wave of nausea hit me. "Can I use your bathroom real quick?" I asked as I clutched my stomach.

Mrs. King nodded and gave me an odd look. "Sure, you know where it is."

I made it to the bathroom in the nick of time. I wondered to myself what in the world was wrong with me. I'd been experiencing waves of nausea and vomiting for over a week.

As I washed my face, there was a knock at the bathroom door.

"Marli, are you all right in there?" It was Chris's mom.

I opened the door. "Yes, ma'am. I think I have a bug or something. I hope I don't give it to Chris or Tiffany," I said and then turned back to the sink.

"Are you sure you're not pregnant," she asked.

I spun on my heels. "What?" I hadn't even considered the possibility of being pregnant. It just hadn't occurred to me. I never felt this sick when I was carrying Tiffany.

She raised her eyebrows. "Well, I assume that you and Chris have been together, you know, *in the Biblical sense*. Could it be possible that you're pregnant?"

I shook my head. "No," I lied. I just couldn't deal with that right then.

"Are you sure?"

"Yes, ma'am. I should go. Chris is already upset."

"Okay, well, we'll be over with Tiffany after a while. We'll call when we're on our way."

"Okay, thank you."

I left the Kings' house and made a stop at the drugstore before heading home to Chris.

TWENTY-THREE

"IN ANOTHER TIME"

I arrived home to find Chris right where I'd left him—sitting on the couch. But now there was a duffel bag sitting on the floor beside him, and he was fully dressed. He'd even shaved.

I stood by the door for a few minutes and tried to get my head together before walking into the living room. "I'm home," I said. "You going somewhere?"

He looked up at me and smiled. It was the first time I'd seen a smile on his face since Russell died. It was a wonderful sight to see.

He stood up and kissed my cheek. "Yeah, I got a call from Herb Gentry. He wants me in his band."

My eyes widened. "*The* Herb Gentry? Of the Herb Gentry Ensemble? I didn't know you knew him. You never mentioned it." The Herb Gentry Ensemble was a world-renowned jazz group known for its soothing, jazz tunes and flawless, live performances in small, intimate venues. It would be an honor for anyone to be chosen to play with them.

"Well, he saw The St. Louis Kingsmen perform in Memphis

awhile back, and he approached me, said he liked our sound. He took my number and said he'd be in touch. I thought he was calling for the whole band, but he just wants me. Can you believe it? He wants *me* to perform with his ensemble."

I shook my head. "All of this happened just in the time I was gone?"

He nodded. "Yeah. Amazing, huh?"

I looked away from him. "So you're going?"

He placed his hands on my arms and laughed. "Well, yeah! Baby, this is the chance of a lifetime. How can I say no? His people have already booked a flight for me and everything. My plane leaves in a couple of hours. I really think this is what I need. I think I'll feel better if I can get away for a while."

I looked down at the floor and wondered what I should do or say at that point.

"What's wrong? You look upset," Chris said.

I looked up at him and blinked back tears. "I'd be lying if I said I didn't want you to stay. I'll… I'll miss you."

He pulled me close to him. "Baby, I'll miss you, too. But I'll only be gone for four months."

"Four months?" I backed out of his arms and shook my head. "Four months is too long."

He frowned. "Too long for what?"

I wiped the tears from my cheek. "Nothing. Go ahead. It's what you wanna do."

"Marli, what do you mean it's too long? Are you saying that you won't wait for me?"

I sat down on the couch. "I don't know if I *can* wait, Chris."

He kneeled in front of me. "What are you talking about? It's only *four months,* baby. I'm no good to you here right now. I need to get away and clear my head, and when I get back, we can go ahead and get married. I'll be able to be a husband to you."

I stared down at my hands in my lap. "What am I supposed to do in the meantime, Chris? I quit my job and I'm miles away from my home. Am I just supposed to sit here all by myself and wait?"

I looked up to see a shocked look on his face. He was quiet. I had a feeling he wasn't sure what to say.

I looked him in the eye. "You haven't even considered me in all of this, have you? You just expect me to say okay and go along with this and sit here in *your* condo and wait for you, don't you?"

Chris sat down beside me. "I… I'm not trying to hurt you, and I don't wanna lose you, Marli. I'm not leaving *you*. I just need to get away for a while. I thought you'd understand."

Tears began to crowd my eyes again. "I *do* understand, but that doesn't mean I have to like it. You don't need my approval, you don't have anything tying you to me, and you don't owe me anything. Just… just go ahead. *Leave.*" *You were gonna do it anyway. Everybody does.*

He placed his hand on my cheek. "Will you be here when I come back?"

I rubbed my finger across his lips and shrugged. "I don't know."

He shook his head. "I don't wanna go unless I know you'll be here when I get back."

"I can't promise you anything, Chris. All I can say is, if we're meant to be together, we'll be together."

He leaned in and kissed me softly. "I love you, Marli."

"I know you do, Chris. I know you do. I love you, too."

He stood from the couch and picked up his duffel bag. I watched as he walked toward the front door and then turned and looked at me. "Please wait for me, Marli."

I looked at him but didn't reply. After he walked out the door and shut it behind him, I leaned back against the sofa and cried like a baby. I should've told him that I might be pregnant. I knew I should've, but I couldn't. I couldn't bear the thought of him sticking around only for that reason. The last relationship of mine that was based on an unplanned pregnancy had ended disastrously. I just couldn't go through that again.

I sat there for most of the night and listened to my phone ring over and over again. I ignored the calls from Chris, Tiffany, Chris's parents, and Carla. I sat there and tried to figure out what to do. *Should I actually stay here in Chris's condo and wait for him? Should I go back to Arkansas? Or should I just leave for someplace else altogether new?* I had enough money saved up to start a new life anywhere I wanted to.

Finally, I left Chris's place and drove to the club where I'd first met him. Disregarding the possibility of being pregnant, I ordered a drink, sat at a corner table, and nursed my sorrows. When a tall, average-looking brother approached me, I let him sit at my table and woo me with a bunch of corny come-ons and pick-up lines. And when he invited me to his hotel room, I readily accepted.

In his room, I let him kiss me and caress me and undress me while I closed my eyes and pretended that he was the man I loved. I tried to feel Chris's touch in this stranger's hands. I tried to feel Chris's lips in this man's kisses. I tried to feel Chris's love through this man's lust. I tried, but I failed. As the man continued on his quest to consummate our one-night union, I gently pushed against him to stop him.

"What's wrong?" he asked in a voice that was not Chris's.

My answer was to grab my purse and excuse myself to the bathroom. I sat my purse on the side of the tub and stared at myself in the mirror. My purse tumbled into the tub, spilling its contents, and as I grabbed my personal items and shoved them back into the purse, I noticed the small drugstore sack. Then I heard Chris's voice echo in my mind: *"You're worth so much more than that."* That's when I snapped out of it. That's when I realized what I was doing.

I clutched the bag and sat on the toilet and sobbed loudly. Jerry or Barry, or whatever he said his name was, knocked on the door and asked me if I was okay, and I just kept crying. When I finally emerged from the bathroom, I apologized to him, redressed, and quietly left the room.

TWENTY-FOUR

"SOMEBODY ALREADY BROKE MY HEART"

I smiled as I walked out onto the back deck of my rented cabin and took a seat at the patio table. I brought my cup of decaf coffee to my lips, took a sip, and opened the newspaper. I took a deep breath and breathed in the cool, March morning air. I'd always wanted to live in Hot Springs, and shortly after Chris left, I packed my things and headed back to Arkansas. In no time, I found a nice cabin located right on Lake Hamilton and moved in. Now, three months later, I remained there—alone, but content.

I looked out across the lake and then down at my growing belly. I never wanted to raise another child alone, but I was actually excited about this new baby. It felt like a fresh start for me in a lot of ways. I would be able to raise this baby without any interference from my family, and that alone made me feel better about the whole situation.

I spoke with Chris's family from time to time, but I hadn't told them about the baby. His mother was especially upset about how things had turned out. After he left St. Louis, he'd grown even more distant from everyone in his family. They barely heard from him at all.

He did manage to call me from time to time, but I never answered. I just didn't see the point. He'd made his decision. After promising to never leave me and begging me to stay with him, he'd left. There wasn't much I felt we needed to say to one another at that point. When the baby was born, I'd tell him because I knew he had a right to be a part of his or her life, but other than that, there was nothing between us except for some beautiful memories. That's all there would ever be between us.

Tiffany was still doing well at Spelman, but she'd changed her major to art history. As it turned out, she'd always dreamed of being a museum curator but was afraid of disappointing me, my father, and the rest of our family. I was thrilled she decided to pursue a career that *she* chose instead of one someone else chose for her.

The unexpected buzzing of my cell phone stirred me out of my thoughts. It was Carla. She and Bryan were still working hard to salvage their marriage, but things didn't look too promising for them.

"Hey, girl," I said.

"Hey! Just checking on you and the little one. How're you feeling? How are things there?"

"We're good. Everything went well at the doctor's yesterday. And I've found a really nice church here, met some great people. I even have a prayer partner now."

"Good. And how are you otherwise?"

I knew what she was getting at. "I'm good, Carla. Really I am."

"Okay…"

"Okay, huh?"

"Well, I just don't understand why you won't tell Chris, that's all."

I sighed. We'd been over and over that subject time and time again. "Carla, I have my reasons. You know that."

"Well, I'm just saying, Marli, the man was in pain. He'd just lost his son. You can't hold his actions against him."

"Carla, I'm not mad at him, and I'm not holding anything against him. I know Chris. If he knew I was pregnant, he'd come right back to me—he wouldn't have left in the first place."

"*Duh*, then why won't you tell him?"

"Because if he comes back for the baby, I'll never know if he really loves me or if he's just with me out of some sense of duty."

"Of course he loves you. You know that."

"Do I? I mean, he left me, remember?"

"Marli, look. You're making this whole thing be about you. Remember how you told me I was being selfish back when I was on that sexual bender in St. Louis? How I was making what Bryan did all about me?"

"Well, yeah, but this is hardly the same thing."

"*Yes, it is.* You're being selfish, only considering your own feelings. It's got to be the pregnancy hormones that have you acting like this. The man lost his child, Marli. *His little boy*. Neither you nor I can even begin to know what that feels like. He couldn't have known how to cope with that. You should've stayed your behind in that condo and been waiting there with open arms for him when he finished that tour. No, *actually*, you should've married him long ago instead of punishing the man for being rich. Who does that? That is just about the craziest thing I've ever seen or heard."

I sighed heavily. "Haven't we been through this? I wasn't punishing him, Carla. And it wasn't about him being rich; it was about him keeping it from me. And besides, I apologized for that."

"Yeah, you did, and now you owe him *another* apology. I'm telling you, he is a good man—one of the best I've ever known. You never should've left St. Louis."

"Carla, I couldn't stay there and wait for him. What kind of relationship would we have if I did that? The future would've been full of cycles of him running away every time things got difficult, and he would've always expected me to stay and wait for him. I can't live like that."

"Okay, maybe you're right, but what are you gonna do, Marli? Raise another baby on your own when Chris is out there and you're still in love with him?"

I opened my mouth to reply and then shut it. There was no use in denying the truth. I *did* still love Chris… and I missed him.

"Uh-huh, you know I'm right. You need to call him, Marli. Or at least answer his calls. And you need to tell him. He has a right to know about this baby, *his baby*."

I closed my eyes and took a deep breath. "Honestly, Carla, at this point I'm scared to tell him."

"Why?"

"Because I'm afraid he'll be angry with me for keeping it from him."

"The longer you wait, the more likely he'll be angry."

"I know… but what if he's so angry he won't want anything to do with me?"

"That'll never happen. I have it on good authority that Chris King is still crazy about you. Call him, Marli. At the very least, put him on child support. Hell, he's rich."

"*Carla…*"

"Okay, okay, I'm kidding. Call him so the two of you can be together again."

"Carla, can I tell you something?" I asked in a tiny voice.

"Yeah, you know you can tell me *anything*."

I released a ragged sigh. "I *do* still love him, and I've wanted to call him. I've wanted to answer his calls, too. I'm just scared, Carla. I'm scared of being hurt again."

"Marli, are you any better off being without him and still loving him? Are you any less hurt?"

"No."

"Look, I almost let my pain over Bryan's cheating cause me to lose not only my family, but my soul. I deserted my own kids, and I was committing more sins than I could keep track of because being in pain can make you do some really stupid stuff. Now, we might never truly work things out, but I love Bryan and my sons enough to try. If you don't pull yourself together, you're gonna lose Chris forever. Don't be stupid. *Call him.*"

"What if it's too late? What if he has someone else?"

"It's not and he doesn't. Call him. As good as he is? You'd be a fool to just let him go."

I nodded as I wiped a tear from my cheek. "Okay, I will. But there's something I need to take care of first. Something my prayer partner and I are working on."

"Don't wait too late, Marli."

"I won't."

"And Marli, you deserve to be happy. Don't ever forget that."

"Thank you, Carla."

~*~

I closed my eyes and followed the directions of my prayer partner, Jeanine, regarding Theophostic prayer. I wasn't sure if it would work, but I was definitely willing to give it a try. At that point in my life, I was willing to give most anything a try.

I tried to remember the very first time I felt like I wasn't good enough—like I was unlovable. I thought back to when I was a little girl, to all of the times my mother and father said hurtful things to me, to all of the times they used my flaws to hurt one another. I remembered the times I was made to feel like I wasn't good enough or pretty enough. I could hear my parents' critical words ringing in my ears. I could feel the inadequacy as it pierced my very soul.

I felt so alone then—so abandoned, so hurt, so unloved. I remembered the little girl that I was then. I could see the sadness in her eyes, feel the sheer loneliness that she felt. I wanted to hug her and to tell her that she was a good girl—that she was good enough for love, that she *deserved* love.

And in that moment, I understood *me* for the first time in my life. I understood why I made the decisions I made in the past. And I understood that I deserved much better than I'd ever given myself.

Then, as instructed, I offered a prayer to God:

"Dear Lord, please take all of the hurt and pain I felt then, and still feel today, and bind it with Your love. Heal the broken pieces of my heart, Lord, and make me whole. Take the lies that the enemy has convinced me are true from my mind.

"The enemy says I am not good enough, but You say I'm good enough to die for. He says I'm ugly, but You say I am fearfully and wonderfully made. He says I'm unlovable, but You say Your love for me endures forever. He says I'll always be messed up, but You say You have forgotten my sins and will never remember them again. He says I have no future. You say You have already made plans for my future—*good* plans.

"Thank you, Lord, for loving me and forgiving me. I will never forget Your truths and I will no longer believe the enemy's lies. In Jesus' name, amen."

I took a deep breath, released it, and smiled.

~*~

It was a month to the day after my conversation with Carla that I finally dialed Chris's number. I was ready to talk to him. I was ready to tell him about the baby, *our baby*. And if he would still have me, I was ready to be his wife.

The phone rang a few times, and then his voice mail picked up. *This is Chris. Leave a message.* The sound of his voice pricked at my heart. It was a voice I'd grown accustomed to hearing all the time. I'd missed hearing it.

After the tone, I said, "Chris, um, it's Marli. Please call me back. Okay, bye."

I laid the phone down and stared at it for a few seconds. *Please God, let it not be too late.* I stood from the table, but before I could take one step, my phone began to buzz. I picked it up and checked the screen. It was Chris. My hand trembled, and my heart raced as I pressed the button to accept the call and put the phone up to my ear.

"Hello?" I said softly.

"Hello? Marli?" Chris replied.

I closed my eyes and sighed. It was all I could do not to cry. He sounded *so good*. "Yeah, it's me."

"Wow, I'm glad you called. We were doing a sound check and I didn't hear my phone. When I saw a missed call from you, I thought I was hallucinating. I can't believe it's really you. Man, you sound good. How've you been?"

"I'm fine. You sound like you're doing better."

"I am. I'm *a lot* better, actually, but I miss you. I'm so glad to hear from you."

"I... I miss you, too. Um, we need to talk. You know, whenever you get a free moment. I know you're busy on the road."

"Yeah, it's kinda hectic, but I'm learning so much from Herb. He's an awesome musician. He wants me to join the band full time."

I gulped. "Oh, well, that's great, Chris. I knew he'd be impressed with you."

"Yeah, thanks."

There was a moment of awkward silence, and then Chris said, "Hey, I talked to my mom the other day and she said you moved back to Arkansas."

"Yeah, Hot Springs."

"You like it?"

"I love it. It's beautiful here."

"I've heard. Look, I really wanna see you, Marli. I wish you would come to the show tonight."

"Um, where is it? I'm really not too big on long-distance driving or flying these days." *Because I'm pregnant.*

"Well, God must be in the plan because we're in Arkansas. Little

Rock. At the Peabody. Will you come? I'll leave a ticket at the door for you."

I looked down at my belly. This wasn't exactly how I'd planned on him finding out about the baby. But then again, I really didn't have a plan for that at all, did I?

Maybe I should just go ahead and tell him now. "Chris—"

"I just wanna see you, and this way we can talk face-to-face. Will you come?"

I sighed. "Um, okay. What time does the show start?"

"Nine. I'm glad you're coming. See you then."

TWENTY-FIVE

"SOLDIER OF LOVE"

Dressed in a knee-length, black, trapeze-style dress and modest, black heels, I entered the ballroom at The Peabody and snagged a table near the back. I surveyed the room, ordered a ginger ale from a passing waiter, and awaited the start of the show.

Twenty minutes later, the sold-out room darkened and was filled with the low murmurs of an excited crowd of jazz enthusiasts. I leaned forward and tried to convince myself that I didn't need to use the restroom when I knew that I did. I decided to try and hold it through the first half of the show. I didn't want to risk losing my table or miss a single note of music, so I gripped my legs tightly together and clapped my hands as the announcer took to the small stage.

"Good evening, everyone, and welcome to a night of smooth jazz at The Peabody!" said the short, stocky Hispanic man. "Sit back, relax, and enjoy the sounds of the Herb Gentry Ensemble!"

I watched as the spotlight spread to reveal the entire band. There were two keyboardists, a drummer, an acoustic guitar player, a trombone player, Herb Gentry, himself, on saxophone, and Chris to the right of Herb with his trumpet. I had to fight back tears when I saw him. He looked good, *very good*—like the sunshine after a bad thunderstorm. His hair now fell to his shoulders and he was sporting a neat goatee. He wore a black suit and black dress shirt—unbuttoned to reveal his toned chest. Around his neck hung a platinum chain and on his wrist, a matching bracelet which gleamed beneath the stage lights.

I wiped a single tear from my cheek and thanked God that the room was dark and that I was too far back for anyone to notice me.

Throughout the first half of the performance, my eyes were glued to Chris. I smiled through my tears as he played his trumpet in his usual way—with eyes tightly closed and his head tilted to the left, almost resting on his shoulder, his right foot tapping in time with the rhythm of the drum. For me, the main attraction was not the famous Mr. Gentry but the beautiful Christopher Ethan King. As I watched him perform, every feeling I'd ever felt for him came flooding back.

Between sets, I hurried to the restroom and found myself at the end of a ridiculously long line. As the line crept slowly along, I leaned against the wall and shut my eyes as I rubbed my belly.

"Are you expecting?" A voice asked.

I opened my eyes and saw that it was the woman in line directly in front of me.

I nodded. "Um, yes, I am."

"Oh, how sweet! How far along?" the petite, older lady asked.

I rubbed my fingers through my now huge and unruly afro and smiled. "Um, five and a half months."

"Well, you look beautiful. You're absolutely glowing."

I smiled again. "Thank you."

"I tell you what, go on ahead of me. I know how it is to be pregnant. I have four children of my own. Of course, they're all grown, and now I have six grandchildren."

I moved ahead of her in line. "Well, you're very blessed."

She nodded. "Yes, I am, and so are you. Your husband must be thrilled."

I only offered her a weak smile in response. Luckily, it was my turn to enter a stall so I just turned and thanked her again and headed to the toilet.

As I walked back into the ballroom and settled into my seat, I didn't notice that several members of the band were already up on stage. I also didn't notice that one of those band members was Chris… and I didn't notice *him* noticing *me*. I sat there quietly, looking around the room at the others at their tables—mostly couples out for a night together—and felt a little pang of loneliness. I turned my attention back to the stage as the sound of microphone feedback filled the room.

"Um, we'll need another five or ten minutes, everyone. Just hang tight," said Herb Gentry.

I watched as he whispered something to Chris and then as Chris left the stage and walked straight to my table. I leaned forward and placed my hands on the table to steady them. My heart hammered in my chest as he stood directly in front of me and stared down at me.

"Hey," he said softly.

The look in his eyes almost made me come undone. He was the same Chris. He looked the same, sounded the same, and smelled the same. And my feelings for him were the same. *I loved him.*

I couldn't take my eyes off of his as he sat across from me at the table. "Hey," I said, barely above a whisper.

"You are altogether beautiful, my darling; there is no flaw in you," he said.

I smiled. "Song of Solomon?"

He nodded. "Chapter four, verse seven." He placed his hand over mine and returned my smile. "You look so beautiful. A real sight for sore eyes."

I shifted my eyes to our joined hands. "Thanks. You look good, too."

"I'm glad you called. It was good to hear your voice. I, um, tried to call you a few times. Never could get you."

My eyes met his again. "I'm sorry about that. I guess I just thought we didn't have anything to talk about."

He raised his eyebrows. "And now we do?"

"Yeah, we do."

"I'm glad you're here. After the show's over, just sit tight. We can go have a drink and talk for as long as you want."

"Okay. Sounds good."

He lifted my hand to his lips and kissed it softly. "I'll see you soon, Mean Marli."

"Okay, Cool Chris," I said with a slight smile.

He leaned across the table and whispered, "And you know this."

My smile widened as I watched him walk back toward the stage with a confident swagger that I knew and loved.

~*~

I sat at my table and thoroughly enjoyed the second half of the show. The band was phenomenal, and Chris was brilliant, as usual. It was emotional seeing him, but I managed to hold it together. At least until…

Toward the end of the show, Herb Gentry introduced the band members one by one, ending with Chris.

"As some of you already know, I love little surprises during my shows, and tonight is no exception. I'd like to introduce to you our newest member, Mr. Christopher King," he said.

Chris stepped forward, held up his trumpet, and bowed. I smiled and applauded along with the rest of the audience.

"Unfortunately, Chris is only with us temporarily, but I'd like to make it permanent. He's highly talented and can play most of the instruments on this stage. *And*, he can sing. Ladies and gentlemen, I present to you a young man I like to call my baby brother. Without further ado, Mr. Christopher King!"

I leaned forward, my eyes glued to the stage as the tall, thin, dark-skinned man handed the microphone to Chris.

"Thanks, Herb. Um, good evening, everyone. This is a song that is a favorite of someone very special to me. Um, it's traditionally sung by a beautiful woman, but tonight, I'm gonna sing it *for* a beautiful woman. I hope she enjoys it. I hope you guys enjoy it, too."

Well, once he began singing "You Love is King," I lost it. I think I cried through the entire song. Chris's clear, tenor voice was absolutely flawless, and the words touched me deep inside my heart and soul. He closed his eyes and leaned his head to the left and played his vocal instrument with such emotion that it took all I had in me not to run up on that stage and hug him and never let him go.

His performance earned him a well-deserved standing ovation.

After the show, I stayed in my seat, just as Chris had requested, and waited for him while almost everyone else filed out of the ballroom. The lady from the restroom wished me good luck and said goodbye just as Chris approached my table.

"Good luck with what?" he asked.

I smiled nervously. "With life, I guess. We met in the ladies room."

"Wow, you must've made some impression on her in there."

I shrugged. "I guess."

He reached for my hand. "Come on, we can go to the bar."

"Wait... um, are they closing down the ballroom already?" I asked, hoping that I could just stay seated. I wasn't quite ready to tell him or *show* him that I was pregnant at that point.

He glanced around the room. "I guess not. You wanna stay here and talk?"

I nodded. "Yeah, that would be great."

He shrugged. "Okay."

He sat across from me and smiled. "I can't get over how beautiful you look tonight. I mean, you've always been beautiful, but there's something different about you. You're *glowing*."

I smiled shyly. "Thanks. Um... Chris, I need to say something."

He shook his head and interrupted me. "Let me go first. Marli, I owe you an apology. Through everything that happened, you stayed right by my side. You were there for me, and I can't thank you enough for that. I hope you can forgive me for leaving like I did. And I know I owe your daughter an apology for leaving before I got a chance to meet her. I'm really sorry about that, too. But at the time, I really thought I was doing the right thing and I guess it really *was* the right thing for me, but I should've handled things differently."

I looked at him and bit my bottom lip. "Um, well, I forgive you. It... it's all right."

"No, I really mean it. There hasn't been a moment since I left that you haven't been on my mind. I've missed you so much. I've missed holding you and touching you. I've missed *loving* you."

"I... I've missed you, too, Chris."

He looked me dead in the eye. "I still love you, Marli. I still love *every inch of you*. I never stopped."

My heart fluttered at hearing that he still loved me, then it sank at the thought of him hating me for keeping the pregnancy from him. "I love you, too, but I need—"

"And if you'll take me back, I wanna try and make things work with you."

"But what about the ensemble, the tour?" I asked.

"As soon as I knew you were coming tonight, I quit the band. This was my last show."

I frowned. "*What?* You gave up an opportunity like that without even knowing if we'd get back together? Chris, that's crazy." *Oh, Lord, he's really gonna hate me now.*

"Then I guess I'm crazy. Look, baby, I'm not gonna lie. Playing with Herb has been like a dream come true. It's been phenomenal to work with such a legend. But it is nothing compared to being with you. You gotta know by now what kind of man I am, what's in my heart. I could tour the world and play in the best venues, and it would mean nothing without you. My life is empty without you, Marli. I love you. You're my perfect fit, remember? I *need* you. How I'ma be the next black president without you, baby?"

I laughed as I felt tears begin to fill my eyes. "Chris, I'm—"

Before I could finish the statement, Chris stretched his long body across the table and covered my lips with his. He kissed me deeply, and I could feel his passion and love for me all the way down to my soul.

He cupped my tear-streaked face in his hands. "I'll do anything to make things right with you. We can get married tonight and live wherever you want to—no more playing house. Just give me a chance."

Through my sobs, I said, "I've missed you *so much*. I should've stayed and waited for you. It's… it's not your fault that things got all messed up. I was *so broken*. All you ever did was love me and make me feel special. You were... you *are* so good and now I know that God sent you to me—to help me heal. To show me that I was worthy of love—real, unconditional love.

"I just... at the time, I didn't know how to accept it. I didn't think I deserved it or *you* for that matter. And... and when you left, I was almost relieved that it finally happened. Because a part of me always expected it to happen. But still, it hurt. In the rational part of my mind, I knew you weren't trying to hurt me. But in my messed up heart, it felt like you deserted me. I had tried so hard to be there for you and to make things work—like I did with my parents and my ex-husband.

"Our relationship was always wrapped up in my past hurts and I'm sorry for that. And I'm sorry that I let my brokenness ruin us, but I've been working hard to fix my problems and with God's help, I'm doing better. I still have a ways to go, though."

Chris wiped the tears from my cheek. "I'm glad you're doing better, baby. Look, I'm sorry for the things your parents and your ex did and said to you, and I'm sorry for what those things did to your self-esteem. But *I love you*, Marlena Meadows. I love you with all my heart. I love and want you because you are beautiful inside and out. You're what I've been looking for my entire life—the answer to my prayers."

"You still want me as jacked up as I am?"

Chris reached for my hand and gripped it tightly. "You are not jacked up, baby. You're just human. So am I. Look, I miss you, Marli. It's like I've been missing a piece of myself without you."

"I really mean that much to you?"

"You mean *everything* to me. You *are* everything to me. Can't you see that?"

"You're everything to me, too, Chris. You really are, but there's something I need to tell you, and I hope you'll still wanna be with me after you hear it."

A concerned look spread across his face. "What is it? Is there someone else?"

I shook my head. "No, there's no one else. Only you. I couldn't have found another you even if I'd tried. Have… have *you* been with someone else?"

"No, baby. *No one.*"

"Okay, um…" I released a nervous sigh. I felt nauseated as I stood from my chair and pulled my dress tightly against my stomach. "I'm pregnant."

TWENTY-SIX

"PARADISE"

"Baby, you awake?"

I smiled and shook my head. "Unh-uh. It's your turn. That sounds like Greta, and if you don't hurry up, she's gonna wake Clark up and then you're really gonna have a problem on your hands. You know you can't handle both of them."

"Aw, you gonna leave me hanging like that? Come on, Mean Marli. We're supposed to be in this together," he whispered.

"Mm-hmm, where were you four hours ago, Cool Chris?"

"You were up with them four hours ago?" he asked, sounding genuinely surprised.

"Mm-hmm, with *both* of them, and you slept right through it."

He scooted closer to me and kissed the back of my neck. "I'm sorry, baby. You shoulda woke me up."

"It's okay. I knew your turn would come. You better go get your daughter before she wakes your son up."

He kissed my shoulder and then headed across the hall to our twins' bedroom.

I sat up in the bed and switched on the bedside lamp. I knew it'd only be a matter of time before Clark followed his older sister's example. I smiled as I listened to Chris talking to Greta. He was a good father, the best I'd ever seen, and I was happy to have been able to give him not one, but two children at the same time. I thought about what Rev. King said on the day the twins were born: "God sure gave Chris double for his trouble." It was true. Chris lost a son but gained a son *and* a daughter.

To say that we were happy together would be an understatement. I was so thankful that instead of being angry with me for keeping it from him, Chris was overjoyed about my pregnancy. In short order, we'd gotten married, bought a house, and become the parents of fraternal twins, Greta Monroe King and Clark Spencer King. Of course, Chris's mom named them.

My relationship with my parents was okay. I'd forgiven them, but no miracle had occurred to make us the close-knit family I once wished for. However, I was now a part of an absolutely wonderful family. I was truly blessed to be a King.

I left our bedroom and walked across the hall to find Chris sitting in a rocking chair, feeding Greta a bottle. I stood in the doorway and watched as he kissed her little forehead. She opened her eyes and gazed up at her daddy as he began to softly sing to her.

After a few minutes, he finally noticed me. He smiled up at me and said, "You came to help me after all, huh? You felt sorry for me?"

I walked over to Clark's crib. "No, I just figured that if I helped you, the two of us could get them back to sleep pretty quickly, and then *we* could go back to bed."

"Ready to get back to sleep? You tired?"

I shook my head. "I said I wanted to go back to bed. *Not* back to sleep, if you know what I mean."

Chris's smile widened as he nodded. "Oh, yeah. I definitely know what you mean, and I'm definitely down with that."

I smiled and shook my head. "You are so crazy, Chris."

"Crazy about you, baby."

I picked Clark up and placed him on my shoulder. "I'm crazy about you, too."

Divorce and/or marital separation hurt everyone involved. If you are currently going through a divorce, or you know of a friend or a child suffering from the effects of divorce, visit:

http://www.divorcecare.org/dc4k

To learn more about Theophostic Prayer, visit:

http://theophostic.com/page12414933.aspx

For information about missing kids, visit:

http://www.missingkids.com/home

To learn more about the author, visit:

http://adriennethompsonwrites.webs.com

To join Adrienne's mailing list, sign up here:

http://eepurl.com/jnDmH

Follow Adrienne on Twitter!

https://twitter.com/A_H_Thompson

Like Adrienne on Facebook!

https://www.facebook.com/pages/Author-Adrienne-Thompson/300208429995218

Follow Adrienne on Pinterest!

http://www.pinterest.com/ahthompsn/

Excerpt from "Epiphany" from

Just Between Us (Inspiring Stories by Women)

I was at a point in my life where I was walking around with the weight of the world on my shoulders. My job was stressing me, my man was stressing me, and my bills were stretching me. I was struggling to hold things together for my three kids. I was fighting what felt like a losing battle against poverty and depression. I had a good job, but with that good job, I had accumulated a pile of bills as I tried my hardest to do with one income what could better be done with two. My head hurt and my back ached from the twelve hours I'd busted my behind working at the hospital and I was more than disgusted with my former husband/baby daddy and his sporadic child-support payments.

This man had already left me with a five week old, two other children, and no job. It had taken time, sheer will, and much help from the good Lord to make it from the pit of depression I fell into after he left, to deal with the heartache and disappointment and humiliation that comes along with a failed marriage, but I had managed to make it through all of that only to land in a new space full of new stressors—single motherhood.

At least I had a decent job and a decent home and my smart, beautiful children were pretty easy to raise, but still there were three of them and only one of me. I was one person dealing with three separate personalities, moods, and quirks. It took two to make them, there definitely should've been two of us there to raise them, but no, I was it. There was just me and the pressure of having to teach my girls to be women and my son to be a man was staggering. It felt like I was carrying a boulder of parenthood around with me day in and day out and my knees were buckling beneath the pressure and the mere weight of the load.

That's where he came in with his looks and his swagger. He wasn't Denzel handsome, but he possessed the strong facial features that had always appealed to me, and he had a way about him that made him stand out in a crowd. He wasn't tall or the best dressed man I'd ever seen. He was just magnetic, and so cool you would've sworn he was Billy Dee's twin brother. The confidence he exuded was almost palpable…

Excerpt from

Been So Long 3 (Whatever It Takes)

Coming early 2014

I hurried through the parking lot to the ER entrance, my feet trying to match the pace of my thoughts, which were racing at breakneck speeds. Thoughts of the possibilities of what I would face inside of that hospital. All they'd told me was that my husband was hurt and in critical condition.

I tried to steady my breathing as I held the bottom of my swollen belly and waddled to the receptionist's desk. I was out of breath as I asked about my husband. Sahib stood behind me, tears streaming down his face. I'd apologized for raising my voice at him, but he'd been dragging his feet back at the house, and we didn't have time to waste. His feelings were still hurt, but I knew he'd get over it. Besides, what was going on with the love of my life was the most important thing in the world at that moment.

"Please have a seat, ma'am. They're working on your husband right now. I'll let you know his status as soon as I hear from the doctor," the receptionist said in a calm, soothing voice.

I wanted to yell at her, to scream that I didn't want to sit down or wait. I needed to see my husband, and I needed to see him *right now*. I couldn't wait. I had to see his face, to know that he was okay. But I looked down at Sahib and then felt my unborn child kick and felt the discomfort I'd been feeling at the bottom of my stomach since I got the news, and I decided to go ahead and sit down for a moment.

I took a seat. Sahib sat down beside me and continued to wipe his own tears and sniffle and hiccup air. I pulled him close to me and hugged him tightly. "I'm sorry, baby. Everything will be okay. Stop crying, sweetheart." I kissed his forehead, and he began to calm a bit. That made one of us. I was still on edge, but I knew I had to keep my cool for Sahib and my unborn child and my husband.

Thirty minutes of worrying and praying passed, and the receptionist finally called my name. She agreed to keep Sahib at her desk for me. As I walked through the ER to Trauma Room Three, I felt my heart race. She'd said my husband was stable but that I would only be allowed to see him for a moment before they transported him to ICU.

I walked into the room and gasped. There he lay—motionless. Machines whirring all around him. His clothes cut to shreds and in a bloody pile on the floor. I slowly walked over to him and rested my hand on his forehead. I leaned over and kissed his cheek and let my tears flow freely.

"Baby, it's me. It's Mona-Lisa. Please be okay, baby," I whispered. "Please be okay. I need you. We all need you. I can't have this baby alone. Please get better. Please be okay. I love you so much..."

"Mrs. Masood?" a nurse said. "We need to take him to his room now. You can visit him there when he gets settled."

I nodded. "Okay, thank you." I leaned over and kissed his cheek. "I love you, Wasif. I'll see you again really soon."

Made in the USA
San Bernardino, CA
04 September 2018